ATHENA

GODS AND MONSTERS: BOOK ONE

Eva Pohler

Book Layout ©2017 BookDesignTemplates.com
Book Editing by Alexis Rigoni
Book Cover Design by B Rose Designz

ATHENA/ Eva Pohler. -- 1st ed.
ISBN: 9798323360932

A wise [person] can be a fool in love.
— **Chetan Bhagat**

Contents

PART ONE: ANCIENT TIMES

CHAPTER ONE

Escape

Warm blood cradled her, though it would be many days before she would have the words to comprehend it.

I am inside my mother's womb.

It was cozy, warm, and soft. She stretched her arms, turned, and closed her eyes, but before she had fallen back to sleep with her knees pressed against her cheeks, a deep voice rang out in a threatening roar.

Her mother's voice, calm and quiet, followed. "I will not destroy the babe."

"Metis, you must, if you love me."

That was her mother's name—Metis.

"I will not."

A pressure disturbed her cradle, followed by sudden jerks of movement and her mother's wail. She clenched her tiny fists and uncoiled herself, ready to spring into action. She flattened her feet against her mother's backbone.

Her mother's screams unnerved her. For many hours, she listened to the distressing sounds and felt her mother flailing against her prison.

"Let me out of here!" Metis cried repeatedly.

Once her mother's cries had subsided and all had gone still, she put her hand against her mother's belly. It was warm and firm. "Mother? Are you well?"

Her mother flinched with surprise.

"Mother? Metis?"

Warm hands pressed the belly from the other side. "I am here, child. All is well."

The sound of something scratching woke her from her slumber. She stretched her tiny fists. "Mother? What are you doing?"

"Tearing splinters from your father's ribs."

Her eyes opened wide, warm fluid coating them. "Why? How?"

"Your father, Zeus, is the king of the Olympians. He swallowed me because of a prophecy that I would give him a son who would one day unseat him."

"I am not a son. I am a daughter, I believe."

"Yes, I believe it, too. I shall call you Athena. My only concern now is setting you free. I shall weave armor for you from these splinters and find a way to get you out."

"I like it here."

"For now," her mother said. "But you are growing, and soon there will be little room. You will become restless and bored, and you will long for something more than this. I must prepare for that day."

"Mother?"

"Yes?"

"I like my name. Thank you for it."

"You are welcome, my precious child. And now, I want to exercise your mind with a riddle."

Athena smiled, ready for the challenge.

Her mother began, "Imagine that your father gifts me a beautiful pear tree. If the main trunk has twenty-four branches, and each branch has twelve boughs, and each bough has six twigs, and each twig bears one piece of fruit, how many plums can the tree produce in one growing season?"

Athena put her finger in her mouth. After a moment, she removed the finger. "The tree can bear 1,728 pieces of fruit."

Metis pressed her hands against her belly. "How wise of you to put it that way, since a pear tree would produce zero plums."

"I thought you may have misspoken," Athena explained.

"It was a trick. If you had said that the tree would produce 1,728 plums, you would have been wrong, because pear trees cannot produce plums, but because you said, 'pieces of fruit,' you bested me, the goddess of counsel!"

Despite the many riddles her mother told her to pass the time, Athena soon outgrew her cradle and felt suffocated by it.

"Let me out of here," she said one day.

"You must find your own way out. I will help as much as I can."

Athena searched for an opening and found one. Her mother bore down as Athena squeezed through, first her head and then the rest of her. When she was free at last, she found herself in another cradle not much bigger than the one she had left, made smaller by the presence of her mother.

Metis embraced her. "Well done, my precious child. Now that you are born from me, you are immortal, as I am. But when you are stronger, you must do that again."

"Will you follow me?" Athena asked, still wrapped in her mother's arms. She pressed her ear against her mother's bosom and was comforted by the sound of her beating heart.

"It is not my destiny. It is yours."

Athena's stomach formed a knot, and tears pooled in her eyes. She would never leave her mother.

For many months, as she doubled and tripled in size, Athena watched Metis weave her father's bone splinters into armor, making beautiful, ornate designs with red fibers stripped from her father's innards. Her mother showed her how to make the weave tight and even.

"Will not my father miss his bone and innards?" Athena asked as she weaved a long splinter in the fashion shown to her by her mother.

"Look around. He is a god. Everything I take grows back within a day."

"Are we also gods?"

"Indeed."

"How did my father come to be the king?"

"Pull it taut, Athena. Here, let me show you."

Metis took the breastplate in her hands and worked her magic. She had created a central floral design and was now developing a chain-link border around the edges.

Athena assumed her mother had forgotten her question, but after a while, Metis said, "Zeus's father, Kronos, was once King of the Titans and ruler of all the earth. Like Zeus, he was told that his children would one day overthrow him. To avoid it, he swallowed each of his babes as soon as they were born."

"Including Zeus?"

"No, he was spared by his mother after she had given up five of her children. She wrapped a stone in a blanket and gave it to Kronos to swallow instead. Then, she hid Zeus in a cave at Mount Ida on the island of Crete, where he was raised by nymphs. That's where I met him. We swam and chased rabbits together. He often sought my counsel. I'm the one who gave him the potion that caused Kronos to vomit his five children from his belly. Zeus was waiting to rescue them. He and I and his mother whisked them away and, together, we made plans for the rebellion that made your father king of the Olympians."

"He was lucky to have you, as am I."

"It's not over yet. While it's true that Kronos has been captured, Zeus and his siblings continue to fight against Titan and Giant uprisings and search for ways to secure their rule. Zeus freed many of his father's other children—Giants born of Gaia, the Earth—hoping they would come to his aid in vanquishing the followers of Kronos. But some turned on him."

"Is my father a good warrior? A good leader?" Athena asked.

"He was until he swallowed us."

"He did it to protect his throne," Athena insisted.

Her mother met her eyes. "You don't resent him for it?"

Athena shook her head. "I would have done the same."

Metis's blue-gray eyes widened with surprise. "So, you are ruthless like your father? I hope in time that you will learn compassion and empathy."

Feeling snubbed, Athena said nothing as her mother continued weaving.

Almost an hour passed before Metis spoke again. "Nevertheless, you must escape. You're fully grown. Even when I make myself as small as I can without compromising my work on your armor, there's little room in here for the two of us. More importantly, you have a destiny ahead of you—adventures and glory beyond your greatest imaginings."

Athena frowned. "Won't you miss me when I'm gone?"

Metis dropped her weaving and cupped Athena's face. "More than you can fathom. Stay close to your father, and you will be close to me."

Athena enjoyed watching her mother weave the armor, and she especially took pleasure in doing it herself, when her mother would allow it. One day, as she watched Metis pull the threads in and out, she studied her mother's face, admiring her beauty. Raven hair fell across her back and blue-gray eyes trimmed with long, dark lashes looked upon her work. Delicate but strong hands moved tirelessly, making intricate patterns in the armor. Athena wondered if she resembled her mother.

She had the same color hair, though it didn't quite reach her shoulders. And her skin was fair. But what of her eyes? Her face?

"Mother? Do I look like you?"

"Indeed, though your eyes are more brilliant—a stunning gray."

Athena smiled and kissed her mother's cheek.

"How about another riddle?" her mother asked.

Athena beamed. She loved the challenge.

Metis cleared her throat. "When called in for questioning, a prisoner is warned by Zeus, 'If you lie, I will throw you into the pit of Tartarus. If you tell the truth, I will swallow you.' What does the prisoner say to save himself?"

Athena tapped her finger to her chin. After a moment, she replied, "The prisoner says, 'You will throw me into the pit of Tartarus,' because throwing the prisoner into the pit would cause a contradiction, since the prisoner would have told the truth. He can only be sentenced to Tartarus for a falsehood. And swallowing the prisoner would also create a contradiction, since the prisoner would have stated a lie and can only be swallowed after stating the truth."

Metis embraced her daughter. "Very good." She drew away and added, "The prisoner might also say, 'I am a liar.'"

Athena shook her head. "My answer is better, Mother."

Metis laughed. "Why is that?"

"Because even liars sometimes tell the truth. If the prisoner says that he is a liar, Zeus could swallow him without contradiction."

"You have bested your mother once again." Metis smiled with glee. Then she asked, "Can you make yourself small, like me? There will be more room."

"I don't know how."

"Visualize it, and it will be so."

Athena closed her eyes and imagined herself small, like a bird. Her perspective changed, and when she looked down at her body, she saw feathers.

Metis chuckled. "You're a little owl. Keep practicing, my love."

When Athena climbed her father's ribs and leaned close to his throat, she could hear his conversations. Over time, she came to recognize the voice of Helios, the sun god, and his sister, Selene, the moon. They reported the movements of Zeus's enemies to him. Athena also recognized the voice of Zeus's new wife, Hera, who bore him two sons. They were called Ares and Hephaestus.

Zeus had children from other wives before Hera and after Metis. The twins Apollo and Artemis proved skillful with the bow and arrow. Hermes was easily the fastest and most cunning of all the deities. Persephone brought springtime everywhere she went. And Aphrodite, according to what others said, was the most beautiful, next to Hera.

There was another voice that Athena thought was the loveliest she'd ever heard. It belonged to a Titan named Prometheus. His deep, melodic voice soothed her and piqued her curiosity.

One day, Zeus announced that he would invite the Giants who had fled to the Caucasus Mountains to pledge their loyalty to him on Mount Olympus.

"They will be grateful for my mercy," Zeus insisted.

Prometheus objected. "If you open the gates, they may strike. Instead, you should invite them to another location where our allies, hidden from view, surround the meeting place. If the Giants charge you, we will be ready. And, if they go down on their knees before you, you should test them before accepting their pledge."

Athena grinned and nodded, whispering, "Well done, Prometheus!"

"Test them? How?" Zeus asked.

"Send them to attack the Titan rebels hiding in the Himalayas. If the Giants succeed in bringing the rebels back to the meeting place as your prisoners, then they will have earned your trust, and you will have killed two birds with one stone."

"Mother, I think you've been replaced as Father's counselor," Athena called down to where Metis worked tirelessly on the armor.

"You might think so, but you are wrong. I often whisper advice to him while he sleeps. He thinks the ideas are his own."

"Why do you wait until he sleeps? Why not speak to him now?"

"He hears better when all is quiet. Besides, it is easier for me to climb to his ear when he is lying flat."

When her father next lay down to sleep, Athena climbed beside his ear and said, "Father, this is Athena, your daughter by Metis. If you set me free, I can help you win the war."

Athena was startled when he mumbled, "Too dangerous for a child. Safer where you are."

"But Mother says I'm full-grown, that gods age differently from one another."

"Let me think on it."

Athena's heart soared.

Months went by without another word from Zeus, and Athena, as her mother had predicted, grew restless.

Metis took her daughter by the shoulders. "Bargain with your father. Tell him that in exchange for advice—advice that will help him win the war—you want your freedom."

"What advice would I give?"

"The Giant Alcyoneus is only immortal in his native land," her mother explained. "Tell Zeus to shoot the Giant and drag him across his borders, where he will die."

Athena did as her mother said, and Zeus was pleased by the outcome.

"Father, now will you set me free?" Athena asked.

"It is not the time, but soon," came his reply.

Athena fumed.

Suspecting that her father knew that the advice about the Giant had come from Metis, Athena climbed higher than she'd dared to go before, reaching into her father's head. She was pleased when she neared his eyes and discovered that she could see the world through them. Determined to offer something indispensable to him for her freedom, she studied everything with an analytical mind. She held onto his skull as he fought Giants and Titans, and she noted which strategies worked and failed. Meanwhile, below her, her mother fashioned a spear.

Athena learned the names of her father's greatest and strongest allies—his brothers Hades and Poseidon and his sisters Demeter and Hestia. Hera was perhaps his most loyal ally of all.

Swift, dark-haired Hermes led a charge into the Mycenean hills where a rebel base was believed to be located. The twins Apollo and Artemis weren't far behind, their long, brown hair flowing in the wind. Each carried a bow and quiver of silver arrows—"Silver Shooters," the twins had come to be called. Ares and Hephaestus flew on either side of their father. Although Athena couldn't see them unless Zeus glanced back, his brothers and sisters were on his heels with Hera, Persephone, and Aphrodite, along with their allies, taking up the rear.

While her mother continued to work below, Athena watched the great battles through her father's eyes with much pleasure. She longed to join her family against their enemies. Artemis and Apollo were indeed experts with the bow. It was a delight to watch Hermes run and fly in circles around the others. And Hephaestus's craftmanship at the forge produced remarkable weapons.

The ally she was most anxious to see was the Titan Prometheus. She was enchanted by the perfect blend of beauty and wisdom he possessed. He wore his dark, curly hair cut short like his beard. Dark, brown eyes gleamed from beneath even darker brows. Like all the gods, his jaw was square, his neck muscled, and his arms ripped with iron bulk. But, unlike the others, she saw unabashed warmth in his smile which, joined with his wise counsel and his stunning beauty, conspired to leave her breathless.

She became consumed by thoughts of Prometheus.

It was while Zeus flew with Prometheus just behind swift Hermes toward the Himalayan Mountains and the Titan rebels that Athena got her first big idea. Prometheus had been right to warn Zeus that the Giants from the Caucasus Mountains would strike rather than bend their knees to Zeus. After vanquishing those enemies, Zeus and his allies were on their way to deal with the Titan rebels themselves.

"Father," Athena said into Zeus's ear. "Tell Hermes to carry a golden jar on his head and, as he nears your enemies, pretend to let it slip that it carries hidden powers of enormous strength. Then order Hermes to lead the enemies into a trap, where your allies will be waiting to ambush them."

Athena held onto her father's skull, wedged between his eye sockets and his brain, as he stopped abruptly in midair.

"I have an idea," he called to Hermes and Prometheus. "Let us return to Mount Olympus to plan a new strategy."

Athena was pleased when the next day the rebel Titans were defeated and thrown into the pit of Tartarus with Kronos and the others.

That evening, as Zeus celebrated with his allies on Mount Olympus, Athena watched gleefully from Zeus's eye sockets, longing to be free to mingle among the party. She enjoyed seeing Prometheus put a golden goblet to his lips as he smiled and joked and sang with the other victors. She longed to touch his cheek and gaze into his dark, intelligent eyes. Her face grew warm with thoughts of him.

"Now, Father?" she asked after he had sat at his throne for a spell to sip a goblet of ale. "Now will you set me free? I can be of more use out there than I can in here."

"You have proven quite useful to me already. I prefer you where you are."

Athena clenched her fists as blood rushed to her cheeks. "But, Father—"

Her objections were cut short when Zeus flattened his palm against his ear, pounding the side of his head, as if he were knocking water loose from the other ear. Athena fell from his skull, slid down his throat, and dropped into his belly.

Metis took Athena by the hands. "Should we make some mischief together?"

Athena wiped her eyes. "Oh, can we? What should we do?"

"Follow me."

Metis led Athena down to her father's bowels, where she jumped up and down, laughing. Zeus moaned, and Athena shrieked with laughter.

"Join me!" Metis said.

Athena leapt onto the colon and bounced, laughing gleefully. Zeus doubled over and hurried to his chamber pot.

Metis and Athena flew up to Zeus's belly and lay beside one another, giggling.

"We got him good," Athena said. "And he deserved it."

Metis squeezed her daughter's hand. "Indeed, he did."

Athena sat up and studied her mother's smiling face.

"What is it, Athena?"

"Why must you stay behind when I am free? I want you to come with me."

"I wish I could."

"Why can't you?"

Tears welled in her mother's eyes. "Believe me when I say that your escape from this prison will be both the happiest and saddest day of my life. But, if I were to follow you, Zeus might turn me into a tree, since I am but a lowly nymph, or, worse, throw me into the pit of

Tartarus where all those horrible rebel Titans and Giants live. He fears I'll have a son who will take his reign. He will never set me free. By staying here, I will be close to you, as long as you are close to your father. I will hear and see you, and that will bring me joy."

Athena embraced her mother, and they cried in one another's arms.

Metis sniffed and added, "As long as I remain in here, I can influence your father. I will do all I can to protect you, my precious, darling Athena."

One night as Athena was thinking about Prometheus, she heard her father at the door to the pit of Tartarus demanding to know where the last of the rebels were hiding.

"Tell me," he bellowed, "and I will set you free."

Athena flew to Zeus's ear. "Is that wise, Father? To set your enemies free?"

"If they cooperate, they are no longer enemies," he mumbled.

"Not true. They may help you in the short term with plans to hurt you in the long term."

"How do you know I'm not bluffing, just to get their cooperation?" Zeus challenged.

"If you do that, your word will mean nothing to them," she replied. "Set *me* free, and I will question these prisoners for you. I know that I can get them to provide truthful answers without promising their freedom."

"What can you do? Silence, child. Do not insult me with your arrogance." Once again, Zeus cupped a hand to his ear and pounded, knocking her from his head, down his throat, and back to his belly, where her mother was waiting.

Athena was on the verge of tears but quickly forgot her frustrations when her mother held up the armor and said, "It is done."

The armor would always be special to Athena. She wore a crested helmet, breastplate, and boots that reached her knees. She also had cuffs to protect her wrists and forearms and a short girdle that gently flared from her waist. Each part of her armor displayed the same intricate design created by her mother of a central flower bordered by a chain-link trim. Made of bone, it was the color of ivory, and the designs were blood-red.

"It fits you perfectly and will increase or decrease in size as you do," Metis said as she looked upon Athena with admiration.

"Thank you. I am pleased and will be forever grateful."

"I wish I had a glass so you could see how stunning you appear."

"I feel powerful in it."

"You are powerful. Here, take your spear."

Athena took the shaft and held it tightly in her fist. "My father lied to me. He will never set me free."

"You will have to find a way out yourself."

She embraced her mother. "Maybe you will follow me some day, if I can convince my father that you are not a threat."

"Maybe."

Athena held Metis tightly, torn between her need to be with her mother and her desire to be free.

"I'll always be close to you," her mother reassured her. "You must go."

"Maybe I should stay a little longer." As much as she longed to speak with Prometheus, she couldn't tear herself away from her mother.

"That will only prolong my pain. I need you out there, living your life."

Reluctantly, Athena flew away from her mother to search for an opening. First, she tried to tunnel through her father's ears, but he stuck his fingers in and blocked her exit. Next, she tried his nostrils, and he did the same. Then, she flew to his mouth and was about to stab his palette with her spear when he drank ale and washed her down his throat and back into his belly.

Although she dreaded it, she swam to his anus, but he pinched his buttocks together so tightly that she could not push her way through.

When she had left her mother's womb, she'd had help, but her father's resistance made a second birth seem impossible. Full of frustration, she jabbed her father's innards with her spear. Although he doubled over, he bore it.

"Father!" she cried with her eyes narrowed and her fists clenched. "I will be free, one way or another!"

Then, she threw her spear with all her might up into his head, where it lodged into his brain.

Her father roared.

Athena raised her brows and met her mother's smile with her own.

"Fly up and push the spear deeper," her mother suggested.

After kissing her mother's cheek once more, Athena rushed to her spear, gripped it with both hands, and drove it into her father's brain.

His roars increased, and he flailed about to dislodge her, but Athena held her footing and kept the pressure on the spear.

Through her father's eye sockets, she noticed gods and goddesses coming to her father's aid. Apollo gave him a concoction to drink. Hestia brought him ice to apply to his scalp. And Hera massaged his temples with oil. But nothing worked, of course.

As Athena smiled to herself, she noticed Prometheus looking into her father's eyes. Up close, his features were even more beautiful and intriguing. She held her breath and studied him, longing to speak with him, to touch him. Then, his mouth opened, and he stared back at her with surprise. Could he see her?

"Lord Zeus," Prometheus said. "You have a daughter from Metis. The only way to end your torment is to set her free." Prometheus turned to Hephaestus. "We need the sharpest axe you have."

Athena's heart raced. Would Prometheus liberate her?

A moment later, Prometheus put his face close to her father's and, looking at her, said, "Stand back."

Leaving the spear in place, Athena flew down to her father's throat just as the blade of an axe split her father's head in two. She glanced down at her mother who was smiling and waving with tears in her eyes. Athena blew her mother a kiss, grabbed her spear, and flew from her father's head, where she hovered above the other gods. Like a wet dog, she shook her father's blood from her skin, hair, and armor.

The great hall on Mount Olympus filled with gasps.

CHAPTER TWO

Prometheus

W ho's this?" Hera cried. A few drops of Zeus's blood had spattered on her vibrant, red hair.

"Zeus's Daughter." Prometheus smiled up at Athena, who hovered above the great hall on Mount Olympus.

"By Metis," Athena quickly added, lest her mother get none of the credit for her birth. "And, as you can see, I'm a daughter, not a son, so I pose no threat to my father. In fact, I've come to help him."

Athena missed her mother already. She fought off tears, not wanting to appear weak before the others. The gods were gathered in the center of the main hall where their intricately carved thrones formed an oval border around the perimeter of the room. Each throne perched on a dais with an ornate door behind it. Above her was the blue sky and the never-ceasing sun she'd heard of—not the same sun as Helios. Below her were floors of marble and columns of gold.

Zeus sat on a double throne with Hera beside him. The throne was decorated with golden birds. Apollo used a needle and thread to sew Zeus's head together again.

When she'd dreamt of her escape, Athena had imagined her brothers and sisters rushing to her side to shower her with kisses of welcome. She'd known even then that it was a fantasy, but she hadn't anticipated the cold stares. Only Prometheus offered her a smile. It was her saving grace.

"And how do you plan to help?" Ares, her brother from Hera, challenged. Like his mother, he had vibrant, red hair and piercing, blue eyes.

Athena straightened her back and lifted her chin. "I have ideas."

The hall erupted in laughter.

"Let her speak," Prometheus shouted. "Give her a chance."

"How can we trust her?" Ares flew to her side and, before she knew what was happening, cuffed her wrists. "She attacked Lord Zeus. That's treason."

Athena attempted to pull free from the cuffs, but the metal wouldn't budge. "What's this?"

"Adamantine," Artemis replied.

Hermes raised a brow. "The strongest metal there is."

She'd heard of adamantine. Zeus had used it on his enemies. Tears stung her eyes. Did her father really see her as his enemy?

Poseidon, whose turquoise eyes were much more stunning in person, explained, "The cuffs will permit you to fly but not god-travel or communicate telepathically."

Athena had no idea what was meant by god-travel or telepathic communication, but she did not ask for an explanation.

"They will also bind you here," Hades added, "to Mount Olympus, for as long as you wear them."

"Is this really necessary?" Hephaestus asked. "We have no reason to believe she's a threat."

"Hear, hear," Aphrodite agreed. "She says she wants to help."

"I want her thrown into the dungeon with someone guarding her day and night, until we know for certain she can be trusted." Zeus held his head between his hands. "It's better to be safe than sorry."

"Hear, hear." Hera sent a mocking glance to Aphrodite.

Athena nodded. "I would draw the same conclusion in your shoes, but I will prove my loyalty to you, Father. You will see."

Ares took the spear from her hand, and she did not try to stop him, though it saddened her, because it reminded her of her mother. When she held it, she felt like she was holding a part of Metis.

With his head mended, Zeus stood up and glared at her. "Cuff Prometheus, too. For all we know, they may be in cahoots."

Prometheus gawked at Zeus but said nothing as Ares placed adamantine cuffs around his wrists, too.

Ares escorted Athena and Prometheus to a dungeon beneath her father's throne. The air hung heavy with the musty scent of damp stone. The flickering light of a solitary torch cast eerie shadows on the brick walls.

"Have a seat." Ares pointed to a bale of hay on the floor and then left, slamming the iron door behind him.

Distressed to learn that she had exchanged one prison for another, Athena sat on the hay. Her prison was made worse by the absence of her mother.

And this was not how she had hoped to become acquainted with Prometheus.

He sat on the stone floor against the wall across from her. His knees were bent, an elbow rested on each knee, and he leaned his head back against the wall. His white tunic was like those of the others— knee-length and tied at the shoulder. He wasn't wearing his usual armor—only leather sandals on his feet.

Now that there were fewer eyes on her, tears slipped down her cheeks. She bowed her head to hide them from Prometheus. "I'm sorry you're in trouble because of me." Athena tried to sound brave.

"This isn't your fault. I'm the reason you and your mother were swallowed by Zeus in the first place."

Athena gasped as fresh tears stung her eyes.

"You must understand, it happened at a time when no one knew who their enemies were. Sharing my vision was a way to prove my loyalty to your father. I didn't know he had already consorted with your mother."

She understood. "I won't forget your help." She removed her helmet and met his gaze.

The air crackled with electricity between them. Was he attracted to her, too?

He smiled warmly. "If you can forgive me, perhaps we might be friends."

She wiped her eyes. "I could use a friend."

He sighed with obvious relief. "Then you have one. I swear on the River Styx that I will help you in any way that I can."

She raised her brows. "You don't even know me."

"I know all I need to know."

Once Athena had adjusted to the fact that she was a prisoner in her father's palace, she was determined to use her time wisely by asking Prometheus questions. From inside her mother's womb, and later in her father's belly, she'd learned much about the world and the beings that populated it, but there were many things she had not learned.

"What did Poseidon mean by god-travel?" she asked after they'd been sitting in silence for a short while.

"It's a form of travel accessible only to the gods. The monsters are incapable of it. Giants can't do it, either. But it's not the safest way to travel."

"What do you mean?"

"Well, the safest is by chariot, because, like our bodies, chariots can be warded for extra protection."

Athena nodded. Her mother had taught her about wards and had even carved two on Athena's body—one on each of her shoulders. The one on her right protected her from being possessed by another deity. The one on her left gave her extra strength and stamina.

"Flight is the next safest," he continued. "And god-travel is the least—though it's the quickest and also the most frequently used."

"But what is it? How is it done?"

"You merely envision where you wish to go, and then you're there."

"Truly? How fascinating. Anywhere in the world?"

"You must be able to visualize it correctly, so you must know where you're going. You must have been there before."

Athena had been to and had seen many places through her father's eyes. "Why is it the least safe?"

"Because for a few seconds after you leave a place, you leave a signature behind that can be tracked by an enemy."

"How interesting."

He grinned. "I suppose there are a great many things you haven't learned."

"Perhaps, but you might be surprised by what I know already."

He chuckled. "I doubt that. You strike me as wise beyond your years."

"I didn't understand Poseidon's reference to telepathic communication."

"Ah. We also call it prayer."

"What is it?"

"Well, you see, if in your mind you address another deity, they will hear it, as if you were in the room speaking to them."

"Truly?" She reached out to her mother but heard nothing in reply.

"It's easy enough, if there are no wards or too great a distance between you and the deity you address. These adamantine cuffs, for example, make it impossible."

"How far is too great a distance?" Athena asked.

"You'd have to be on the other side of the world, in most cases. The more powerful the deity, the greater the distance that can be reached."

"Do you think once these cuffs are off, my mother might hear my prayers to her?"

"I doubt it. Zeus's wards would likely prevent it. But you never know. It couldn't hurt to try—though I'm sure she won't be able to get through to you."

Athena sniffled.

He moved across the room and sat near her feet. "I'm sorry. That was insensitive of me."

She quickly wiped away her tears. She didn't want him to think her weak and pathetic. "I need to know these things. Thank you for explaining them to me. It's truly gracious and generous of you."

Athena saw much more than his generosity. She saw the kindness in his heart. The warmth in his smile. The vitality in his soul. He was breathtaking, and she struggled not to reveal the effect he was having on her.

"It's the least I can do," he said, "considering I'm responsible for your mother's imprisonment."

She found it easy to forgive him for that, even though her heart ached for her mother. "You did what you had to do."

Prometheus leaned forward. "I have a question, too, if you don't mind."

"Ask it."

"In the great hall, you said that you have ideas for ways you might help your father. Would you mind telling me about them?"

"Not at all. For one, I would advise my father to share his responsibilities with his siblings."

"In what way?"

"He should divide the earth into realms, and he and his siblings should draw lots to determine who would oversee them. He would still be the lord of all, but delegating responsibilities will make him a stronger king."

"Indeed."

Although she did not need Prometheus's approval to know that it was a good idea, his approval nevertheless was important to her. She wanted to impress him as much as he impressed her.

"Do you think Zeus will agree?" she asked.

"Let us hope so." He gave her a wink.

Her heart fluttered.

"Was there more?" he asked.

"I noticed something while trapped behind my father's eyes. The power of the gods increases when they are loved or feared. Zeus saved his siblings from their father's belly, and they are grateful. That gratitude contributes to my father's greatness."

"How were you able to draw this conclusion?"

"When someone complimented Aphrodite's beauty, she appeared stronger. When someone praised Hermes for being fast or cunning, he was made more so. The twins with their arrows—the more often they were called 'Silver Shooters,' the more capable they became. Have you not seen it?"

"I'm thoroughly impressed by your powers of observation and by your keen mind."

Athena blushed.

"Have you observed anything like that with me?" he asked.

"Your wisdom and foresight. You were right about those Giants who'd been hiding in the Caucasus Mountains."

"You know about that?"

"I had nothing to do but listen from my father's ears and watch from his eyes."

"Foresight, huh?"

"It's your greatest gift. I even told my mother you'd replaced her as my father's counselor."

Prometheus laughed. "That was my goal, though I now feel quite guilty for it."

"Let it go . . . please."

"So, tell me. After making these observations, what idea came to you?"

She stood up from the bale of hay to stretch her legs. "Why not increase the power of my father and his allies by creating a race of people whose primary purpose is to worship us? This could give us the power we need to subdue any threat to my father's reign."

Prometheus was silent for many seconds before Athena prodded, "Do you not agree?"

He cocked his head to the side as he looked up at her. A chill of pleasure ran up her spine from the sight of his beauty. She wanted to touch his beard, to feel his arms.

Prometheus brought her from her reverie. "It would certainly be good for your father's reign, but what of the race of people?"

"What do you mean?"

"If they are to be made, they mustn't be mere servants to the whims of gods. They must be allowed to pursue their own happiness. And, as their makers, we would be responsible for them. It's not something we should do in haste."

Athena's heart bloomed. If she had thought highly of him from afar in the belly of her father, it was nothing compared to what she thought of him now that she was with him, face to face. "Wise words. My mother once warned me that I was ruthless like my father and needed to learn compassion and empathy, which I believe she has since taught me. But I must say, you are the most selfless being I have ever heard of." She wanted to add that his selflessness was what most attracted her to him—aside from his kind eyes and luscious lips.

"You can't have heard of a great many beings, having just been released from your prison only to wind up in another."

"Oh, but I have. I saw everything my father saw and heard everything he said, along with what was said to him or near him. Believe me when I say I have seen enough to recognize that your selflessness is rare."

Prometheus grinned and looked at her again from head to toe. "I thank you. I learned it from my mother, too."

"Who is your mother?"

"Clymene. Your mother's sister."

Athena gasped and covered her mouth.

"Athena?"

Her fingers began to tremble as her idea of Prometheus shattered. She couldn't believe he would betray his own aunt. "You gave up your mother's sister? Metis was something to you, and you gave her up to Zeus?"

"Athena." He climbed to his feet. "I didn't know she was pregnant. I didn't know he would swallow her."

She began to pace, wildly gesticulating, the anger moving down her arms and through her fingertips. "You should have known there would be consequences. Just the temptation to Zeus would have been enough for him to do what he could to keep them apart." She had once agreed with her father's decision to swallow her mother, but she'd learned a lot since that day. How could Prometheus endanger his mother's sister?

"Athena, wait." He tried to take her hands with his, though they were cuffed together at the wrists, like hers.

She pulled away and continued to pace. "I thought so much of you, I was half in love with you, but you're no different from the rest."

"Athena, please. Your mother advised me to. I shared the prophecy with her and my mother before I told Zeus."

She stopped pacing to look at him. "Are you a liar? I didn't take you for one."

"No. I speak the truth."

"Why would my mother advise you to tell Zeus?"

"Unlike me, she knew that she was pregnant."

"I still don't understand." Athena searched his eyes, trying to make sense of it.

"My mother later told me that Metis feared that Zeus would swallow her child as soon as it—you—were born, and she couldn't bear it. Believing you were a son, your mother wanted the chance to birth you, nurture you, and make you strong inside the belly of Zeus so that you might one day fulfill the prophecy."

"But I was a daughter." Athena bit her lip.

"Yes." His eyes moved over her again.

A chill of pleasure shot up her spine.

"Do you think your prophecy will come to pass?" she asked. "Because if so, that would mean that one day my mother will—"

He quickly put a finger to her lips with one hand and to his own with the other. As much as his touch awakened her senses, the implication of it overshadowed everything. Did he truly believe his mother would escape and bear a son that would unseat her father?

Athena returned to the bale of hay where she sat, covering her mouth.

Prometheus kneeled on the stone floor at her feet. "Did I hear you say that you were half in love with me?"

Her face burned. She averted her eyes. "I can't believe I said that out loud."

He lifted her chin with a finger and gazed into her eyes. "When I first laid eyes on you inside your father's head, I had another vision—one of you and me."

Her eyes widened and her mouth dropped open. "You did? What did you see?"

"This." He leaned in close and pressed his lovely lips to hers.

When he drew his face away and gazed down at her, she looked up at him, somewhat bewildered.

"Do that again," she insisted.

He chuckled. "Happily."

Unfamiliar feelings embraced her from every direction, and a warmth—a heat—took possession of her chest—of her entire body. Of their own accord, she looped her arms around his neck, and her hands, despite the cuffs, reached for his curly dark hair, ran fingers through it, grabbed fistfuls of it. Without her intending it, a moan escaped her lips. Tears flooded her eyes. She had lost control of her body.

His large hands tenderly cupped her chin. She liked the way his beard tickled her lips, her cheeks, her neck. She enjoyed the way his tongue explored her mouth, her ear, her throat. She couldn't remember feeling such pleasure.

Time lost its relevance in the passing days as Athena savored Prometheus's kisses. She desperately wished her hands weren't cuffed together, so she could more easily feel his every muscle, explore with her fingers every inch of his flesh.

Their connection deepened with each kiss, as if the world around them had melted away, leaving only the sensation of the other's presence.

So, when Ares appeared at the end of the week to escort them to the great hall above them, Athena wasn't ready to leave the dungeon.

Would Prometheus still want her outside of their prison? Or had he been using her to pass the time?

CHAPTER THREE

Gaia

A res led Athena and Prometheus from the dungeon to the great hall where many of the gods were gathered and visiting.

Zeus stood on his dais. "Give us the room, please."

The other deities, including Hera, exited through the doors behind their thrones, leaving Ares, Athena, Prometheus, and Zeus alone.

Athena felt Prometheus close behind her, his breath on the back of her neck, his hand on the small of her back.

To Ares, Zeus said, "Remove the cuffs and take them with you. Prometheus, you're free to go. I wish to speak to my daughter alone."

Prometheus flashed Athena a gentle smile before he disappeared.

She immediately missed his presence—his breath on her neck, his hand on her back. He hadn't been gone for more than a second, and she longed for him again.

Prometheus? Athena reached out to him telepathically. *Can you hear me?*

Indeed, I can, Athena.

She wanted to ask when she would see him again, but she didn't want to sound needy and insecure. She also doubted he would know. *You were right,* she said instead. *This is easy enough.*

Good luck with your father. He can be a bully, but he can also be kind.

Zeus stepped down from his dais to stand before her. "My spies informed me of everything you said to Prometheus. I feel confident that you are, indeed, my ally."

"Thank you, Father." She was hoping for an embrace but was afraid to make the first move.

"You may call me 'Father' when we're alone, but in public, I want you to address me as 'Lord Zeus.'"

She gave a little bow. "It shall be done." She wasn't hurt—not much, anyway. It was wise to maintain formalities in public.

"Since you are now without a mother," he began again, "I want to take you to meet someone who might be there for you when you have questions that I, as a father, might not be able to answer."

Athena wasn't sure whether to be pleased or annoyed. Was he truly wishing to help her? Or was he passing her off to someone else?

Besides, she wasn't without a mother. He wasn't aware of it, but Athena could still see Metis waving at her from behind Zeus's eyes. It brought her immense comfort.

"Follow me," he instructed.

He led her from the palace temple, across the golden-paved courtyard, and into the stables. They passed six different stalls, each containing a magnificent beast, before stopping at a seventh.

As Zeus bridled the black stallion, he said, "This is Boreas, the north wind. He and the south, east, and west winds pull my chariot. Here, take his reins while I bridle the others."

"It's nice to meet you, Boreas," Athena said to the horse.

The stallion nodded and whinnied his reply.

Athena was pleased by how gentle Zeus was with the horses. He stroked their coats and spoke to them softly. To one of them, he said, "Zephyr, that shoe needs fixing," before he tapped on the hoof and magically repaired the shoe.

With all four bridled, Zeus led Athena and the horses to an outbuilding across from the stables, where the chariots of the

Olympians were parked. He hitched his golden chariot to the horses and helped Athena climb aboard.

"Take the reins," he said as he climbed in beside her. "You should learn how to drive one of these."

Athena's hands trembled with excitement. "What command shall I give them?"

Telepathically, he replied, *To the omphalos.*

"To the omphalos," Athena repeated.

All at once, the horses took off from the outbuilding and flew through the gates into the open sky above Greece where Helios was just beginning his ascent from the east.

As they flew south, Zeus pointed. "That's the Aegean Sea to our left, the Ionian to our right, and Mount Ossa below."

Athena already knew their names, but not wishing to appear ungrateful, she said nothing while taking in the beauty around her.

It was one thing to see the world from behind her father's eyes and another altogether to see it firsthand. The sky seemed bluer, the seas more turquoise, and the land in richer hues of green and brown.

"This is amazing," she said simply. Then, turning to him, she asked, "Why are we going to the omphalos? And what is it, exactly?"

"It was the stone my mother gave my father to swallow in my place." He told her the story Metis had told her about Kronos swallowing each of his children before he was given a stone swaddled in a blanket in Zeus's place. "We call it the omphalos—or bellybutton— because of its location. Years ago, I sent two eagles to fly in opposite directions, and I watched carefully to see where they would cross. That intersection is where I chose to place the stone, and it has since been considered the bellybutton of the earth, the bellybutton of Gaia."

"Are we going there to visit Gaia?" Athena asked with wide eyes.

Her mother had told her many stories about the primordial being who was the embodiment of the earth and the mother of almost every other being in existence.

"Yes, we are. I often visit her for council, and in addition to introducing you to her as your surrogate mother, I want to ask her if she's seen the last of the Giant rebels."

"Why would she betray her own children? Though, I suppose you are her grandchild, right?"

"Right. And so few remain of the Giants that she wants to be in my good graces, knowing my victory is virtually complete."

"Do you know how many remain at large?"

"No more than a dozen, I believe. And while no single Giant poses a threat to us, if they were to join forces, they could overtake enough of us to gain leverage."

"I see."

The horses and chariot zig-zagged between a few more mountain peaks before beginning their descent.

"I'm glad the horses know where they're going," Athena said.

"You're a natural at the reins. Too many drivers want to control the horses more than is necessary."

Athena smiled. It had been her first compliment from her father. It made her long to please him again, so she might gain another.

"By the way," he began. "I couldn't help but notice that you are quite fond of Prometheus."

Athena felt the blood rush to her face as her cheeks grew warm, even with the cool wind beating against them. "Yes, I admire him very much."

"I worried you might have . . . questions," Zeus said awkwardly. "You must know that I love my wife Hera with all my heart. To my eyes, she is the most beautiful and interesting of partners. However, she is also the most jealous, and I fear she would not advise you without attempting to come between us. She's jealous of anyone who loves me, even paternally. I considered asking Demeter to counsel you, but she's singularly focused on her own daughter, and I fear she would neglect you. And although Aphrodite is an expert when it comes to matters of the heart, I believe your siblings may feel some jealousy of you and possible unease over my attempt to bring you into the fold."

Athena took a deep breath, impressed that he had put so much thought into his choice of a mentor for her. "So, Gaia it is."

"Precisely." He gave her a warm smile.

Athena quickly added, "I don't know how Prometheus feels about me. I don't know if what happened between us was anything more than a way to pass the time."

"And only time will tell," he said gently. "However, I must admit that my feelings for Prometheus changed somewhat when I learned that it was at your mother's bidding that he revealed the prophecy about her son one day deposing me."

Athena nodded. "I understand. I guess that means we are both feeling unsure about him."

The horses and chariot circled Mount Parnassus before landing on a hillside at Delphi.

"Here we are," Zeus announced. "Oh, I meant to ask . . . where did you get your armor? It's magnificently made. Its fine craftsmanship matches that of Hephaestus."

"My mother made it from your bone splinters and innards."

He lifted his brows with surprise as he climbed down from the chariot. Athena followed, trying to stifle her smile.

"Gaia's cave is this way," he said. Then, he added with a chuckle, "I suppose I protect you in more ways than one."

She laughed at his joke as she followed him through an opening in the hillside that led into winding caverns carrying them deeper into the bowels of the earth. The tunnels were dry and dusty and full of loose sand and rock. Athena spotted a snake slithering away from their path, and there was something else that disappeared between small rocks—perhaps the snake's dinner.

"Greetings," came a voice.

Athena squinted. A figure came out of the darkness glowing like an ember. She had long, auburn hair, dark brown eyes, and dark bronze skin.

"Greetings, Gaia," Zeus replied. "May I introduce you to my daughter, Athena?"

Athena liked the fact that he referred to her as his daughter. She smiled at the bronze goddess and gave her a low bow.

"Greetings, Athena," the goddess said with a nod and a smile.

"Hello," Athena said. "It's a pleasure to meet you."

Gaia turned to Zeus. "To answer your question about the Giants, Enceladus is hiding in a cave near the Messina Strait, and Typhon is in a cave near the peak of Mount Etna. The others must be at sea, for I cannot sense them."

Zeus and Athena exchanged eager glances. Athena was ready to prove herself to her father by taking on the Giants.

"And to answer your question about Prometheus," Gaia continued, "he is the most noble of the Titans, but any who love him must have strong and enduring patience."

Athena wanted to ask the goddess what she meant by that but didn't wish to seem ungrateful.

"Thank you, Gaia," Zeus said with a bow. "If you learn of the whereabouts of the other Giants—"

"You must come to me, Zeus. I will not tattle on my children unprovoked."

"Fair enough."

Before either Zeus or Athena could say more, the earth goddess disappeared.

Athena then realized that Gaia had not answered Zeus's questions out of love or loyalty; she had done so begrudgingly, almost as if she had little choice.

As they made their way back through the winding tunnel toward Zeus's chariot, her father said, "I'm sorry she wasn't very motherly. That was rather a disappointment."

"I don't need a mother." She hoped her mother knew that what she meant was that she already had one. "I've got you, right?"

He flashed her a smile. "Indeed, you do."

"Where should we go first? The Messina Strait or the peak of Mount Etna?"

"That's the spirit, Athena. But shouldn't we recruit the other Olympians to help us?"

"Not if we attack the Giants one at a time. You can count on me, Father."

CHAPTER FOUR

Hunting Giants

The crisp sea breeze tousled Athena's hair as she held the reins of Zeus's chariot after having commanded the four winds to take them to the Messina Strait. She said nothing to her father concerning what she'd surmised about Gaia and the earth goddess's motives for speaking with them. Athena was wise enough to know that some things were better left unsaid.

When the Messina Strait finally came into view, unfurling before them like a blue ribbon beneath the rising cup of Helios, Athena scanned the coastline in search of the Giant Enceladus.

"He'll be expecting us," Zeus warned. "Gaia will have told him we were coming."

With a pounding heart, Athena gripped the reins, determined to prove herself to her father.

As they descended toward the rugged cliffs of Italy, the earth trembled below them. She tightened her grip on her spear as the Giant emerged from his cave, a colossus wreathed in shadows, his eyes ablaze with fury.

"You were right," Athena said. "He knew we were coming."

"Perhaps I should take the reins?"

"I've got this, if you don't mind."

Athena directed the four winds down toward Enceladus, circling him overhead, until the Giant appeared dizzy.

"Well done," her father remarked.

Enceladus waved his massive fists in the air with anger. Then, Athena handed the reins to her father, and, gripping her spear, leapt from the chariot.

She danced around Enceladus, her spear a blur of silver in the sunlight to anyone who might have been watching. Overhead, Zeus let loose a series of axes hurled with precision at their target. They lodged in the Giant's body but did nothing to deter him. Athena searched for the Giant's weakness, for every blow she'd managed so far had not seemed to slow him down. She'd gouged one eye, but it had not slowed him down. She'd punctured his breast, but he'd swatted at her like a fly. She'd pierced his thigh, but he hadn't even limped with the wound.

As she neared his throat, a mighty sweep of his hand sent Athena sprawling, her body crashing to the rocky coast. Pain flared through her limbs, and she dropped her spear, but she grabbed it up again, gritted her teeth, and flew to meet her foe.

With renewed determination, Athena gouged out the other of the Giant's eyes before driving her spear through one ear and out the other. She was alarmed when this did not kill him. As she retrieved her spear from his brain, he blindly swatted at her with his fists, nearly knocking her down again. She flew like a bee around him, avoiding his blows. Her father attempted to move in closer, prepared to launch another axe, but the Giant got lucky when one of his fingers caught in the mane of Zephyr and hurled the chariot toward the sea.

Full of frustration, Athena grabbed hold of the ground beneath them, her muscles straining with the effort. With a mighty heave, she lifted the island of Sicily from its foundations, the land trembling in her grasp. Enceladus fell from the coast and into the Messina Strait.

"Father, fly toward the mainland!" Athena warned, the island of Sicily heavy in her hands.

Zeus commanded the horses away from the strait just as Athena hurled the island on top of the Giant. With a deafening crash,

Sicily swallowed the Giant whole. Athena watched as the waves crashed and the sand settled, and the only thing remaining of Enceladus was a lone fist reaching toward the sea. It hardened into the cliff edge and became a part of the landscape.

She flew down to make sure he was dead. Hermes met her there. He'd come for the Giant's soul, which would be returned to the Fates.

"He's gone, then?" she asked him.

"Dead and gone," he assured her. "You were most impressive."

"You saw?"

"We all did." He pointed to the sky overhead where some of other the Olympians had gathered to watch.

"We're headed to Mount Etna now," Athena said to Hermes. "Typhon is expecting us."

"Especially now that you've shaken the whole island to its core," Hermes said with a wink.

As if on cue, Zeus approached in his chariot and cried, "Jump in!"

Athena left Hermes to rejoin her father.

"Well done, Athena," Zeus said as he handed her the reins. "Just brilliant."

She smiled widely and said to the four winds, "To Mount Etna."

The chariot turned toward the tallest mountain of Sicily, its peak still intact but obscured by billowing clouds of smoke and ash not more than a hundred miles away.

The clouds parted, giving the chariot a clear path to the mountain peak. Athena was surprised not to see Typhon among the cliff edges.

"He's probably waiting to ambush us inside his cave," Athena theorized.

"You may be right. Pull over there, and we'll enter his dwelling together."

Normally, she would not advise entering the dwelling of an enemy. Better to lure him out. But she was anxious to please her father, so she lowered them to the mountainside near a copse of trees that would shield the horses and chariot from view. Then, she and Zeus flew to the mouth of the cave, the other Olympians waiting above, ready to be called into action.

The labyrinthine caverns reminded her of their journey to see Gaia, but whereas those tunnels had been arid and dusty, these were humid and thick with the acrid scent of sulfur.

It wasn't long before they stumbled upon the entrance to a vast cavern, its yawning mouth beckoning them into the darkness. Athena's grip tightened around her spear as they cautiously stepped inside, their footsteps echoing off the rocky walls.

She sensed him before she saw him, his footsteps reverberating in the cavern behind them. She and Zeus must have passed him as he stood still and silent, hiding in the rocky walls of the cavern. Athena turned to face him.

Typhon towered before them, the eyes on his many heads ablaze with anger. His scaled skin was coiled with snakes, and more of them slithered from his many hands, some of which seemed to breathe fire, for puffs of smoke and flame shot out from different directions.

Athena backed away.

With lightning speed, Typhon lunged toward her, his massive hands slashing through the air and shooting flames. Athena barely had time to raise her spear before the force of his blow sent her sprawling to the ground, her breath knocked from her lungs.

Pain exploded throughout her body as she struggled to regain her footing. Just as Typhon was about to deliver another blow, her father flew in front of her brandishing a shield. The shield reflected the monster's fire back at him, hitting him squarely in the chest. Typhon released an ear-splitting shriek as his massive body fell with a thud onto the cavern floor.

Athena drove her spear into his heart, to make doubly sure he was dead, when a rock fell on her head and nearly knocked her out.

The weight of the Giant's fall had quaked the mountain, and now rocks that had been set in the caverns for centuries were jarred loose and caving in on them.

Undeterred, Zeus raised his mighty fist, and with his other hand he circled Athena's waist. Then he forced their way through the mountain until they emerged from its peak in an explosion of rock.

The other Olympians applauded when they saw the victorious duo. The four winds met them in the air above the debris. Athena was at first embarrassed that she'd been bested by the Giant, but the others cheered her and Zeus all the way back to Mount Olympus.

Once they were home, Zeus sang her praises to those who had not witnessed their triumphs. Then he called for a feast, and they celebrated together, making Athena feel, for the first time, like she was part of the family. But, when she glanced around the room, she was disappointed not to find Prometheus among them.

She was about to reach out to him telepathically, but then thought better of it. If he was interested in her, let him prove it.

CHAPTER FIVE

A Race of Men

I'm intrigued by your idea of creating a race of men to worship the gods," Zeus said to Athena as they ate their celebratory meal.

She had never tasted food that had not first been eaten by Zeus. Her mouth rejoiced with the new flavors and textures. Sweet fruit, crunchy vegetables, and hearty, roasted meat proved a sensual delight nearly as pleasurable as Prometheus's kisses.

"I'm happy to serve you, Father."

"I have already given Hephaestus my stipulations, and he has begun forging clay with fire to create the first man."

Athena tried to keep the shock from showing in her expression as she swallowed her bite of crusty bread. "Would it not be wise to proceed with caution? If we're hasty, we're prone to error."

"Are you questioning my judgment?"

She was, but she supposed she wasn't meant to. At a loss for words, she gazed up at her father with a blank look on her face then quickly took a drink of her ale.

"When you're finished with your meal, join Hephaestus in his forge behind his throne and oversee his creations. This new race of men must be weaker than the gods and less intelligent, to never pose a threat; but they must be strong and wise enough to survive. It's a delicate balance, and you must help Hephaestus discover it."

She gave him a nod before glancing around the room for Hephaestus. Not finding him among them, she quickly finished her plate and then flew toward what she hoped was the forge behind what she believed was Hephaestus's throne. She tapped on the door and opened it.

"Hello?" she called out.

The entrance was flanked by two towering flames that danced wildly in their cauldrons, stoked by magical bellows. The flames, along with the glow from a vat of molten lava, cast shadows throughout the room where chunks of raw metal were strewn beside chariot parts and pieces of half-finished armor. Athena stepped inside to find enormous anvils standing like sentinels, each bearing scars of countless strikes. Tongs, hammers, and axes lay on a long, wooden workbench, along with a half-formed lump of clay. Beautifully crafted weapons and armor were affixed to the walls. In the center of the room were the god Hephaestus and three deities whom Athena did not know. They were small, old, and female. All four looked at her when she entered.

Although Hephaestus had a slight hunchback and limp and wasn't quite as beautiful as the other male deities, he was stunning beside the three old hags now studying Athena with scrutiny.

"I'm sorry to intrude," Athena quickly said. "My Father—Lord Zeus—told me to find you, to help with your creation of a race of men."

"Ah," Hephaestus said with a nod. "I'll be right with you."

As Hephaestus returned to his conversation with the three old deities, Athena glanced around the room and, forgetting her resolve to let him make the next move, she reached out to Prometheus, *Can you believe my father has already enlisted the help of Hephaestus to make a race of men to worship us? I tried to point out the risk in such a rash decision, but he became offended and sent me to the forge to help.*

Athena noticed a lovely golden chair against the wall to her left and made her way to it.

One of your father's greatest flaws is his impulsiveness, Prometheus replied.

She clicked her tongue and took a seat in the golden chair.

"Not there!" Hephaestus suddenly shouted.

Athena tried to stand up but found herself trapped. "What's happening to me?"

Hephaestus went to her and sighed. "That's a trick chair I made for my mother, to pay her back for flinging me from Mount Olympus after I was born. It's why my back is hunched, and why I walk with a limp. I never recovered."

As Athena struggled against the power of the chair, trying to get up, to no avail, she asked, "Why would a mother do that to a son?"

"She claims she believed me to be a monster. At any rate, I've lost the key. I suspect Hermes has stolen it. Sit tight for a while, and I'll ask him. The Fates must take priority for now."

He returned to his conversation with the three hags.

So, they were the Fates, Athena thought, as she listened in on their conversation with immense curiosity.

"No matter how you fashion them," one of the old deities said in a throaty voice, "their bodies will eventually expire like the other beasts."

"Though their souls will live on," one of the others clarified.

Hephaestus scratched his head. "If their bodies expire, we need them to propagate to replenish the population, yes?"

Athena raised her hand. "Might I suggest you wait and see how the experiment goes before making them capable of reproducing?"

The craftsman nodded. "Wise thinking." He turned to the Fates. "What say you?"

"Begin with the male," one of them said. "I will spin the thread of life."

"I will weave it," the middle one rasped.

"And I shall cut it when the time comes," said the third.

Athena reached out telepathically to Prometheus. *At least Hephaestus listens to my counsel.*

When Prometheus made no reply, she reached out to him again. *Prometheus?*

Worried that he had become annoyed by her chatter, she refrained from further attempts. Instead, she bit her lip and worried that he did not love her.

After the Fates had left the forge and Hephaestus had gone looking for Hermes, Athena was surprised by the appearance of Prometheus.

"That explains it," he said when he saw her in the chair.

"Explains what?"

"Why you never answered me." He ran a hand through his curly, dark hair. "Who trapped you here? Hephestus?"

"It was an accident," she said. "He's gone looking for the key."

"He shouldn't leave it out in the open like this."

"I doubt there's anyone else who would sit on it."

"Even so."

She noticed how agitated he was—clenched fists, pursed lips, and rocking back and forth on his feet.

"Are you worried he won't find the key?" she asked him. "Or is something else bothering you?"

A soft chuckle escaped his lips as he shook his head.

"Prometheus? What is it?"

He turned to the half-formed clay on the workbench. "He's using clay?"

"The Fates are helping. Apparently, they are each the spinner, weaver, and cutter of the threads between the body and the soul."

"Did they not offer gifts to these new beings? My brother, Epimetheus, was given the task of distributing gifts from the Fates to the beasts of the land. He didn't anticipate that new beings would be made. I don't think there are any left. This race of men will be naked and defenseless—without fur, flight, speed, or strength."

"Perhaps we can give them language," she suggested.

"We'll make them upright, like us." Prometheus glanced at the two towers of flames dancing near the entrance. "And give them fire."

She watched him repeatedly comb his fingers through his hair, clearly agitated.

"You're worried," she pointed out. "You think Zeus is making a mistake."

"What?" He turned to face her. "No. I'm not thinking about the new creations."

"Something is weighing on your mind."

Prometheus gave her a bashful smile and shook his head again. "Oh, Athena. Earlier, I confessed my feelings to you, and when you said nothing back to me, it frightened me to the bone."

"You did what?"

"Is it better that you didn't hear?" he asked, still standing a distance from her.

Before she could reply, Hephaestus returned holding a key. "Here we are. I was right about Hermes. He only gave in when I told him that you were stuck." He turned to Prometheus. "Hello, what brings you to my forge?"

As Hephaestus unlocked the chair, Athena glanced at Prometheus, but he avoided her gaze.

"I've come to help with the creation of the new beings."

"Lovely," the craftsman said with a hint of sarcasm. "Shall we get started?"

Prometheus shaped the clay into bodies resembling his. Hephaestus forged the clay with fire. And Athena breathed life into the forms to animate them, instilling them with intelligence and the power of language. Hermes was called in to transport the new creations to the caves near the base of Mount Olympus. Two by two, the swift god flew down with the men until a tribe of thirty had been established.

The Olympians then flew below and spent several months teaching the men how to survive, though the gods dimmed themselves because their true form was too much for the mortals to behold. Athena taught them language and showed them how to weave fibers into clothing and blankets. Demeter taught them to plant gardens and harvest crops. Prometheus gave them fire and showed them how to use it. Hephaestus taught them how to make tools and weapons. Artemis and Apollo showed them how to hunt with bows and arrows. Hestia taught them to cook. Hades, Ares, and Poseidon taught them how to build shelters and ships.

Zeus was pleased, so he ordered Hephaestus, Athena, and Prometheus to make more tribes of men, and he came to call the people "humans," which meant "men of earth."

But it wasn't long before the gods realized that the bodies of the men easily expired, and the souls, though immortal, lacked the ability to worship the gods. So, Zeus consulted with the Fates, who directed him to bring the souls to the Underworld, where they would remain for eternity. Souls belonging to men who had been good would spend their eternal life enjoying the illusions of the Elysian Fields. Souls belonging to those who had done evil would be tied to rocks in Tartarus and left to suffer. Zeus assigned Hermes the role of collecting the souls.

During this time, Athena and Prometheus had been too busy to talk about their feelings for one another, and Athena was anxious to have time alone with him. However, she hadn't slept in many months and soon realized she had no place outside of Zeus's belly to lay her head. Therefore, when the gods returned to Mount Olympus to take a break from their tasks with the humans, Athena decided to pull her father aside before their meeting to ask about a room of her own. As she neared Zeus's throne, she heard him complaining to Prometheus.

"Metis is inconsolable. She is crying a river, sending me to my chamber pot more often than I wish."

"Stay close to Athena," Prometheus suggested, "and your problem will be solved."

As Prometheus left her father's side, he turned and smiled warmly at her. She was pleased with his advice to her father. Her heart blossomed with love for Prometheus. Again, she wished for time alone with him, to hear what he had said to her while she was trapped in Hephaestus's trick chair, and to tell him what was in her heart as well.

Before Athena reached her father, a throne emerged on a dais from the marble floor to his right, between his double throne with Hera and the throne of Hestia.

"That is yours," Zeus said to her. "And your rooms shall be beside mine."

A door appeared behind her throne.

"You may furnish and decorate them as you wish," he said. "But I've already taken some liberties because I know you must be tired and in need of sleep."

She resisted the urge to embrace him or to call him "Father," since there were others about, but she did manage to kiss his cheek.

"Thank you, Lord Zeus." When she gazed into his eyes, she saw her mother smiling and waving. Tears slipped down Athena's face as she smiled back at her mother. "I love you so much."

Zeus thought her words and tears were meant for him and seemed genuinely touched. "Darling daughter, it gives me pleasure to make you happy."

Then, she hugged her father, for she was bursting with joy to have the love of both parents.

"Stay close to me," he said.

"It would be my greatest honor," she replied.

She sat on the throne to her father's right and held her head high. She was an official member of the Olympian council. Even Prometheus didn't have a throne to sit on.

Zeus returned to his seat and lifted his arms. "Your attention, please. We have much to discuss before we rest."

The other gods took their seats—those with thrones. Others—loyal Titans and servants to the Olympians—stood along the perimeter of the room between the thrones. Prometheus stood between Athena and Hestia. On the other side of Hestia, Hecate sat on a stool beside Demeter and Persephone's double throne. Iris, a small, winged goddess of the rainbow and a messenger servant to Hera, hovered in the air between Hera and her son, Ares. A group of nymphs, called the Charities, sat at Aphrodite's feet. Another group, called the Muses, gathered beside a golden harp behind Apollo.

"I have decided to divide the earth into three realms," Zeus began. "My brothers and I will draw lots to determine which of us will rule the skies, the seas, and the Underworld, where our new race of men will dwell in death."

Athena straightened her back. This was the second of her ideas that her father was using to secure his reign.

The three Fates—the spinner, weaver, and cutter of the threads of life—flew in from the main corridor each with a roll of parchment in her pale, wrinkled fist. Hades, Poseidon, and Zeus stepped from their thrones to meet the old deities in the center of the room.

Athena covered her mouth with delight when the old hags began to dance in a circle, waving their arms in the air. They switched places in line and twirled around. After a few minutes, they stopped before each brother, holding out the roll of parchment.

The brothers took their lots and opened the scrolls.

Zeus smiled victoriously and lifted the scroll in the air. "The skies!"

Poseidon too was smiling wide when he declared, "The seas!"

Only Hades wore a frown. He said nothing as the three brothers returned to their thrones.

The Fates brought forth a gift to each of the brothers.

One flew to Zeus with a lightning bolt, bright and formidable. "Use with care. One jolt from the bolt will paralyze a deity and destroy a mortal."

A second flew to Poseidon with a three-pronged trident sizzling with electricity. "To balance the power between you, this too will paralyze a deity and destroy a mortal."

A third flew to Hades with a helm.

"This hardly seems fair," Hades complained. "My brothers receive gifts of great power, and I get an iron helmet?"

In a raspy voice, one of the Fates replied, "This is the helm of invisibility. Its wearer cannot be seen by any but us."

Hades lifted his brows with surprise. He placed the helm on his head and vanished. The hall filled with sounds of awe.

When the meeting had ended, Athena turned to Prometheus, who was already waiting for her.

"Can we talk?" she asked.

"I was about to ask the same of you."

"Come with me to my new rooms."

Athena led Prometheus through the ornate door behind her new throne and was pleased by what she saw—soft couches, a golden table and chairs, a cozy fire in a stone hearth, and running water that pooled into a basin along the back wall. But she was even more pleased when Prometheus drew her into his arms and, without hesitation, kissed her.

"I want to know what you said while I was in the trick chair," Athena insisted with a smile.

CHAPTER SIX

Treason

Athena and Prometheus spent as much time together as possible over the next several months, though it was never enough given the amount of attention required by the humans. When the gods weren't teaching their new creations, they were overseeing them to ensure their survival. For the latter, Athena turned herself into an owl and watched from treetops. Prometheus, who loved the sea, became a dolphin who followed men in their ships.

Zeus transformed into a hard task-master, insisting that the new race of men thought themselves on equal footing with the gods. His obsession with keeping the humans down grated on Athena's nerves, but there was nothing to do but obey her father's commands. Unsolicited advice from her had backfired more than once.

His focus had shifted from finding the last remaining Giants to putting the humans in their place. At a council meeting one morning, he declared that they would meet with the original tribe to institute a tradition of sacrificing to the gods.

Zeus further explained, "Each time they kill a beast, they will offer some of it to us, to show their gratitude and humility."

Prometheus raised his hand. "I volunteer to create a demonstration. During it, you can show them the portion owed to us."

"Very well," Zeus replied. "Have it ready by tomorrow's evening."

Prometheus bowed to Zeus, and Zeus ended the meeting.

After they'd retired to Athena's rooms, Athena said to Prometheus, "I did not expect you to help my father in his desire to institute a sacrifice."

"It's good that I can still surprise you after being together for nearly a year. You know what else is surprising?"

"Tell me."

"That I have never taken you to meet my mother or to see where I live when I'm not here with you on Mount Olympus. Would you like to go with me now?"

She grinned with delight. "Indeed, I would."

They borrowed her father's chariot, and she drove across the bright sky to the east, to a mountainous island in the East China Sea where the water ran into the mouth of a shallow cave.

As Athena parked along the bank, a golden goddess emerged from the water and flew to a glowing hearth to dry herself. She wrung out her long, golden locks and looked upon Athena with curious golden eyes as she and Prometheus entered the cave.

"Hello, Athena."

"You know who I am?" she asked.

"Of course, I do. You're the only thing my son talks about these days."

Athena gave Prometheus a bashful grin. "It pleases me to hear it."

"Hello, son. You've been gone too long."

"Hello, Mother. Are you well?"

"As well as one could be when two of her sons are suffering."

"Suffering?" Athena turned to Prometheus.

"My brother Atlas was condemned by Zeus to keep Uranus from mating with Gaia, or Mother Earth. He stands on a mountaintop holding Sky on his shoulders. Another brother, Menoetius, is in the pit of Tartarus."

Athena sucked in her lips.

"Have you come for a reason?" Clymene asked her son.

"I want to talk behind your protective wards. I don't wish to be overheard on Mount Olympus."

Athena frowned. "I don't understand."

"Please come and sit by the fire." Clymene beckoned them to the couch.

Athena took a seat, but Prometheus remained standing by his mother.

"I want to tell you about my plan for tomorrow's demonstration," Prometheus explained. "I'll kill an ox and divide it into two equal portions. One portion will contain the meat and another the bones. Which portion do you suppose your father will ask to be given to the gods?"

"The bones. The people would starve if he were to choose the meat," Athena pointed out.

Prometheus ran a hand through his curly, black hair. "Yes, but I will wager he will choose the meat anyway."

"You don't think highly of my father."

"I think he regrets the new creations," Prometheus said. "He sees them as a threat rather than as a support to his reign."

"But they're defenseless against the gods," Athena argued, even though she knew Prometheus to speak the truth.

"Allow me to prove my point to you tomorrow night. I will cloak good meat in the ox's stomach sack, and I will cloak the bones in glistening fat."

"You will trick my father into choosing the best portion for the gods and condemn humans to starve."

"I don't think so," Prometheus said. He turned to his mother. "What do you think?"

"I agree with my son. Zeus will choose the glistening fat."

Athena was not happy with Prometheus. "If you don't condemn humans to live on bones, you will make a fool of my father. Neither scenario ends well."

"I want to ensure that humans get the better portion of the kill." Prometheus sat beside Athena and brushed her hair from her eyes. "If Zeus chooses the meat, I will suggest that it is only the ox's meat that must be sacrificed. The meat of any other beast is to be eaten by humans."

Athena unclenched her jaw and relaxed. "Fine then, for I have faith in my father to do the right thing."

"And yet," Clymene began, "when he divided his kingdom into realms, he excluded his sisters from drawing lots."

"There weren't enough realms to go around," Athena said defensively.

Prometheus stood up beside his mother. "Ah, but he could have asked the Fates to present six scrolls, three of which were blank."

"Instead, he snubbed them," Clymene added.

Athena climbed from the couch. "Perhaps I should return to Mount Olympus."

Prometheus crossed his arms. "Perhaps you should."

Athena lifted her brows with surprise. Would Prometheus not accompany her? She harrumphed, pivoted, and returned to the chariot without another word.

Athena fumed as she drove toward Mount Olympus. Why must Prometheus provoke her father? Prometheus had said he wished to ensure the welfare of the people, but his trick depended on her father's selfishness.

Although she'd never been introduced to Helios, she waved to him absently as he passed overhead in his golden cup just before the horses reached the gates. After she unbridled the animals and gave them some hay, she returned to the great hall. Most of the gods were gone, probably back helping the villagers. Not wanting to sit around and stew over Prometheus's plans to trick her father, she decided to take her owl form and spy on everyone—the gods and humans alike.

Her heavy heart was lifted as she perched in a tall tree and watched the men celebrating a good harvest together. They didn't always express goodwill toward one another, but this afternoon, they were filled with it as they shared a feast and sang songs—Apollo had taught them to sing.

After their bellies were full, and they were tired of their songs, the king invited his fellow men to join him in prayer to thank the gods for their blessings. Athena was moved and in that moment was glad the gods had created humans. Their gratitude filled her with warmth and a sense of purpose. She hoped never to let them down.

The next evening, Athena was shocked when the Olympians visited the same village, and, during Prometheus's demonstration, her father chose the bones covered in glistening fat. Prometheus had been right about her father. He had chosen what he believed to be the better portion for himself.

The king of the village lifted his hands in the air and announced, "Henceforth, we will keep the meat for ourselves and burn the bones and fat as an offering to the gods."

Athena watched her father struggle to hide his rage. It was one thing to be tricked, and altogether another to be tricked in the presence of mortals. If Athena could have believed her father would choose the fat and deprive the people of nourishment, she would have tried harder to talk Prometheus out of his demonstration. But she hadn't believed Zeus capable of it.

When she glanced across the crowd at Prometheus, he was gloating.

Zeus must have noticed, too, for he unleashed his rage by taking the fire into his great hand.

"You will burn nothing without fire," Zeus said just before he and the flame disappeared.

In the darkness, Athena locked eyes on Prometheus, who was no longer gloating. In fact, he appeared chastened to his core.

As the humans bemoaned their new reality, she went to him. "The humans won't survive without fire. This is your fault. You must do something."

"Let's try to reason with your father. Come on."

They chased after Zeus, who flew in a whirlwind of anger to every village stealing back the gift of fire. She and Prometheus couldn't overtake him, and he refused to answer their prayers. They passed Selene flying across the night sky in her silver chariot. The moon goddess looked down at what was going on and shook her head and clicked her tongue. She, too, was aware of the tragic toll the loss of fire would have on the people below.

When Zeus finally returned to Mount Olympus, he went straight to his chambers, leaving the other gods in the great hall, speechless.

Athena turned to Prometheus and whispered, "What can be done?"

"I can only think of one thing."

She followed him to Hephaestus's forge, where he grabbed one of the two cauldrons of fire near the entrance.

"What are you doing?" Hephaestus, who had not gone to the meeting at the village, called from his workbench.

"Zeus took fire away from our creations," Prometheus explained. "I'm giving it back."

"That's treason," Athena warned. "There must be another way."

"Many humans won't live through the night without the warmth and protection of fire," Hephaestus pointed out.

"You're with me, then?" Prometheus asked the craftsman.

"Can I have more than a moment to think on it?" Hephaestus replied.

"There's no time to lose," Prometheus insisted. "I must hurry before Zeus tries to stop me."

"What will prevent him from taking the fire from humans again?" Athena asked. She wasn't angry with Prometheus but worried about the consequences of his actions.

"His pride," Hephaestus said. "But don't think there won't be consequences—and they might be worse than robbing the people of fire."

"I can think of nothing worse." Prometheus flew from the room, taking the cauldron of fire with him.

Athena exchanged worried looks with Hephaestus. For a god with the gift of foresight, Prometheus was severely lacking.

"I have a bad feeling about this," she said.

"You and me both, sister."

She gave Hephaestus a solemn smile. Even under the circumstances, it felt nice to be called "sister."

Athena waited in her room for Prometheus to return. She prayed to him to come to her chambers rather than stay the night at his cave on the East China Sea. She was worried that Zeus would throw him into the Titan Pit as soon as he discovered what Prometheus had done. She was worried that this would be their last night together.

It didn't take him long to join her on the couch before her cozy hearth, the flames a stark reminder of the sacrifice Prometheus had made for their new creations. And that's what it had been, Athena decided. It wasn't lack of foresight. The Titan knew exactly what he was doing. He simply cared more for humans than for Zeus—or for himself.

Prometheus may have been wrong to provoke her father, but her father's reaction had been worse—it had been evil. The people did not deserve to be punished for Prometheus's trick.

"A father's job is to protect," Prometheus said, echoing her thoughts. "We—you and me and Hephaestus—are the mother and fathers to this race of men. They depend on our protection."

"I know."

"Zeus chose to swallow your mother and her unborn child rather than give up his reign," Prometheus continued. "But he should have been willing to raise his son—or daughter—to take it from him. Zeus should have been proud of passing his reign to his child. I don't want to be the kind of father that Zeus is, don't you see?"

Tears bloomed in Athena's eyes. Her throat felt tight. "Yes."

"Promise me that no matter what happens to me, you'll defend our people."

She met his eyes as tears slipped down her cheeks. "I promise."

"Oh, Athena." He cupped her face and kissed her. "I'm sorry. I should have known better than to test your father. I really was thinking of the people, though."

"Let's not talk about that now."

He kissed her again. She could never get enough of those kisses.

"If he swallows you, I will follow," she said against his lips. "I would be happy to spend eternity there with you. I'll have my dear, beloved mother with me, too."

"No. I wouldn't let that happen." He squared himself to her. "You can't throw your life away by resigning yourself to a prison, no matter who occupies it with you. You have a great destiny ahead of you. I've seen bits of it, of you leading warriors to battle, of you defending a great city. You must live your life and fulfill your fate, even if it is without me."

Athena wrapped her arms around his neck, fighting her sobs. When she could speak, she said, "I know I said I wouldn't lie with you because I was not ready to become a mother, but I've changed my mind. If I must lose you, I want a child to remember you by."

He lifted her chin with his finger and smiled down at her. "No, Athena. I wish I could give you that parting gift, but I cannot make a child knowing I must abandon it."

Athena wailed into her hands.

"Shh. There, there. We don't yet know what my sentence will be. Perhaps your father will be forgiving."

"I will pray to him when the time comes. I will bargain and beg and do everything I can to seek his forgiveness on your behalf."

The possibility of her father's forgiveness comforted her. She lay against Prometheus in the corner of her couch and stared at the fire. She spent the rest of the night hoping.

CHAPTER SEVEN

The Condemned

A thena knew the moment her father had discovered that fire had been returned to the villagers. Through the walls of her chamber where she'd fallen asleep on the couch snuggled against Prometheus, she heard Zeus bellow, "Who has done this? Prometheus? Was it you?"

Prometheus gave Athena a somber half-smile as he peeled her limbs from him and reluctantly returned to the great hall. She quickly followed.

"Yes. It was I," Prometheus confessed. "As you must know, the people cannot survive without fire."

"How dare you?" Zeus raged from where he stood in the middle of the room. "How do you know I wasn't planning to return it at my discretion?"

"It would have been too late for some," Prometheus pointed out.

"And it would have been an effective lesson." Zeus's red face paled to its natural color as he regained his composure and crossed the room to his throne. "Olympians, take your seats and hear what I have to say."

Hera turned to Iris, the small, winged goddess of the rainbow. "Summon Poseidon from the sea and Hades from the Underworld. Make haste!"

Iris vanished.

The others were already there. Demeter and Persephone sat on their double throne with the Titaness Hecate perched on a stool beside them. Apollo, who had been conducting his choir of muses, put an end to the lovely singing and moved to his throne. To his right sat swift Hermes, and to *his* right stood Ares glowering at Prometheus.

Artemis and Aphrodite flew in from their rooms and quickly took their seats. Hephaestus emerged from his forge and gave Athena a solemn nod.

Not long after, Hades, holding his helm of invisibility, appeared with Iris. Poseidon, soaked and dripping with sea foam, soon followed.

Once all were seated, Zeus said, "An act of treason has been committed against me by the Titan Prometheus."

Everyone stared at the Titan standing in the center of the room.

"How do you know this?" Hades asked. "What has happened?"

"Prometheus returned fire to the humans," Hermes replied.

"He confessed," Ares added.

Zeus continued, "First, he set me up to look like a fool before the mortals. Hephaestus, you weren't there, so you may not know what I'm talking about. Prometheus wrapped the meat of an ox in its stomach and warded it, so it appeared to be nothing but innards. The bones he wrapped in glistening fat. Then, he asked me what should be offered to the gods. I chose the fat. The innards, while not tasty, should have been sufficient for our inferior suppliants. They owe their existence to us, after all."

Athena glanced at Prometheus whose fists were clenched at his sides. He avoided her eyes.

"But the Titan had other ideas," Zeus went on. "Either he loves mortals more than us, or he enjoys bringing me down a notch. Either way, he must pay."

"What do you have in mind, brother?" Poseidon wanted to know.

Zeus crossed his arms. "I wish to set an example. He needs to suffer daily for this act against me—against us."

Athena prayed to Zeus, *Father, I beg you to be merciful. Prometheus was thinking of the welfare of the people. He—we—feel protective of them because we made them.*

Zeus glowered at her before addressing the room, "As your leader, I deserve respect—not back-stabbing treason, no matter the motivation. I need you with me, not against me. And I need you to trust me, not undermine me."

"Hear, hear," Hera cried.

Athena prayed again, *If you won't be merciful for the sake of Prometheus, who has been your ally against Kronos and his own race and who has advised you wisely as you've secured your regime, then do it for the sake of your daughter who loves you and who also loves Prometheus.*

Zeus turned to her and lifted his brows but said nothing to her personally. Instead, he addressed the room again, "The pit in Tartarus isn't punishment enough."

Athena added, *Strong kings are models of forgiveness. It will not weaken but strengthen the admiration of others.*

"No," Zeus continued. "This crime deserves something different."

Athena tried once more to appeal to her father. *Show him mercy, and I shall serve you all my days.*

You shall do that regardless, came Zeus's reply. Aloud, he said, "I want something visible, a spectacle that will be a reminder to any who might be thinking of undermining me."

Athena flew to her father's feet and knelt before him. "I beg you to take a day or two to think on this before you act. What harm is there in that?"

He looked down at her with disdain, but behind his eyes, there was her mother blowing kisses.

"I love you so much," Athena mumbled.

Zeus's face softened. "Athena, return to your seat, or if this pains you too much, you may be excused to your chambers."

Athena wouldn't dare leave Prometheus to face his punishment alone. She returned to her throne.

"From this day on," Zeus continued, "Prometheus will be chained to the highest rock on Mount Ida where, each day, my eagle will come at sundown to devour his liver."

Athena covered her mouth to stifle a cry that was choking her throat. Prometheus finally met her gaze with an ashen face.

"If any god kills my eagle or interferes in any way with this punishment, he or she will be condemned to the Titan pit in Tartarus." Zeus added.

The hall filled with whispers as a white-haired god whom Athena did not know flew to Zeus's feet and bowed before him.

"Punish me instead. I have already lived a very long time, but the boy Prometheus has not."

Who is that? Athena prayed to Prometheus.

Aether. He's been like a father to me.

On Aether's heels came the cloud nymphs known as the Nephelae. They were sobbing uncontrollably, raining all over the marble floors.

"Rise, Aether," Zeus commanded. "No one will take the traitor's place. Return to your cave at the top of your mountain, and stay out of our affairs, or you'll see yourself in the pit with your sons."

As Aether stood, shaking and pale and unable to look at Prometheus, Zeus added, "That goes for you Nephelae as well. Leave us. Return to the skies."

Once Aether and the cloud nymphs had gone, Zeus stood. "Ares, get the chains."

Athena could not contain her sobs as she followed the other gods to the island of Crete and up the slope of Mount Ida. They were led by Zeus who held the chains that bound his prisoner. The chains clinked ominously in the wind when the procession reached the highest peak. Prometheus shook so fiercely that he could barely stand. Clymene, her golden hair gleaming like shiny, dancing ribbons, was waiting, her face filled with hatred for the other gods.

She narrowed her eyes at Zeus. She hadn't come to beg, she'd come to threaten. "Don't do this."

Ignoring her, Zeus commanded Hephaestus to use a hammer to stake the chains to the rock. The pounding of the hammer against the adamantine echoed for miles around them. Helios was about to make his final descent. Then, the eagle would come.

"Stop this madness!" Clymene cried.

As Athena awaited the cruel spectacle that would soon unfold, she reached out and took the hand of Hephaestus. Besides her, he alone understood the sacrifice the Titan had made. Hephaestus squeezed her hand gently and gave her a comforting nod.

Telepathically, he said to her, *It will soon be over.*

She knew he meant to comfort her, but she replied, *It will never be over.*

He squeezed her hand again. *One day at a time.*

Aphrodite surprised her by taking her other hand. The goddess, like her, was weeping.

I feel your broken heart, Aphrodite said to her.

Athena gave her a sorrowful nod of thanks, but it was to Prometheus that she prayed, *Be strong, my love. We will endure this together.*

When the moment arrived, and Zeus's eagle descended, Athena averted her gaze. The piercing cries of Prometheus mingled with those of Clymene, along with the shrieks of the eagle, were nearly unbearable, but she knew she had to be strong. She dropped the hands of the other deities and flew to Prometheus just as the eagle ripped its beak through the Titan's side. She beat her breast and wailed so strongly that she injured her throat. Prometheus's eyes and mouth stretched open, but he no longer made a sound as blood spurted from him and the eagle burrowed more deeply into him.

The eagle's head soon resurfaced with the liver in its beak. Prometheus flailed his arms and swung his head violently from side to side before collapsing. The creature devoured its prize quickly. Then, it flew off into the sunset. Prometheus lay still as stone while the gods—even Zeus—wept.

Only Athena, Clymene, Aether, and the cloud nymphs remained with Prometheus through the long, dark night. They worked together to shoo away the wolves and other scavengers as his body healed.

When he awoke in the morning, they cried with him and comforted him as best they could. The cloud nymphs took turns bringing fresh rainwater in a cup, which Athena put to his parched lips. Aether left and returned with a bowl of nuts and a roasted leg of lamb.

"I can't eat," Prometheus said.

"You need your strength," Clymene argued. "Take it, son, please."

They didn't speak much that second day, but as Helios began his final descent in the west, the anxiety in the air was palpable. When the eagle came into view on the horizon hurling toward them like a ball of fire, all save Prometheus wept. Athena's heart raced with anticipation, and involuntary moans escaped her throat as the bird approached. The Titan closed his eyes and steeled himself. He made no noise, no wails, unlike the day before. Although the others shrieked and beat their breasts, he didn't move until the end, when the eagle's beak resurfaced from his side with its prize. Like before, Prometheus flailed his arms and swung his head violently from side to side before fainting in a pool of his own blood.

Athena and the others cleaned him as soon as the vicious bird had gone. Then, once again, they waited with him, protecting his body through the long night.

The days turned into weeks. Prometheus had begun to insist that his supporters go and live their lives.

"If you're condemned, so am I," Athena said.

"Hear, hear," Aether said, his long, white hair and long, white beard blowing in the wind. "We will not leave you."

One day Hermes, whom Athena had not seen since that first terrible night weeks ago, appeared on the rock beside them. Helios was still at high noon, so the anxiety had not yet thickened the air.

"I've come to summon you to Mount Olympus," Hermes said to Athena.

"Why?" she asked.

Hermes scratched his beard. "If you must know, Hephaestus needs your help."

Athena turned to Prometheus. "I'll return as soon as I can." She kissed his cheek and flew away with Hermes.

It was strange to be back at the Olympian palace where deities went about their business as usual, as though one of their friends wasn't suffering in the most dreadful agony every evening. Apollo directed his choir of muses, Aphrodite and her Graces arranged flowers in vases, Artemis had gone hunting, Poseidon and Hades had returned to their new realms, and Hephaestus was hard at work in his forge.

"Hello, Hephaestus," she greeted as she entered. Only one cauldron remained near the entrance with its dancing flame. She wondered what Prometheus had done with the other one after he'd given fire to each of the villages. "I was told that you needed my help."

He shrugged. "Zeus desires it, not I, though I am happy to see you."

"Likewise." She clasped her hands together and rocked back on her heels, anxious to get back to Prometheus. "How can I help? What are you working on?"

He hunched over his workbench sculpting clay that resembled a human. "The first female."

Athena gawked.

"Zeus says it's time," the craftsman added. "And each of us have been asked to endow her with gifts."

"I was hoping we would wait and assess the progress of the villagers before helping them to make more. It won't be as easy to end the experiment once reproduction is made possible."

"It's not for me to question."

"Fine. I shall give her wisdom."

"Zeus forbids it. It's your skill at weaving you're to give."

"Nothing more?"

"Perhaps you can make her a dress?"

"I must hurry if I'm to make it back to Crete before sundown."

Hephaestus frowned but said nothing.

Helios was already descending in the west when Athena rushed to the top of Mount Ida. Prometheus was quiet, having already steeled himself for what was coming. The others were also quiet and somber. They no longer wept and wailed and beat their breasts. They'd come to endure it, silent as stones, like Prometheus.

After the eagle had gone and Athena and the others were cleaning its unconscious victim, Clymene asked about Athena's summons to Mount Olympus.

"Hephaestus was ordered by Zeus to make the first female human," Athena explained. "And we were to give her gifts. I gave her the skill of weaving and sewed her a silver dress." Against her father's wishes, she had also given wisdom, but she would not admit this aloud, lest her father hear of her treasonous act.

"Fine gifts, indeed," Clymene said as she rubbed a wet cloth along her son's arm. "Not like the others."

Athena looked up from her own cleaning to meet Clymene's gaze. "What do you mean?"

"I was told that after Aphrodite gifted the female with grace, Zeus ordered her to add a cruel longing that would never be satisfied."

Athena's jaw dropped open. "But why?"

"That Zeus is a piece of work," Aether complained.

"That's not the worst of it," Clymene continued. "Hermes was told to give her the skill to tell convincing lies with crafty words."

Athena jumped to her feet. "Unbelievable. Where did you hear such horrendous things?"

"From my sister Dione. She heard it from her daughter, Aphrodite."

"But you've never left this mountaintop," Athena pointed out. "And I've not seen your sister here."

"We speak to each other continuously though prayer," Clymene said. "I shouldn't have to tell you that."

"I'm sorry." Athena blushed. "I'm grasping at straws, unwilling to believe my father capable of such injustice. To design the female race in such a way as to cause nothing but conflict and pain for themselves and others is beyond my comprehension. I must go and put a stop to this at once."

She kissed Prometheus, who still lay unconscious on his rock. As she turned to leave, she noticed Selene was flying overhead in her silver chariot. Athena flew up to speak with her.

Even in the distance, Athena could make out the goddess's long, silver hair and how it fanned out behind her, as did her long, white, luminous robe. Her robe formed a crescent at the collar, tied at her throat. Two silver horses, with manes as long and iridescent as hers, pulled her chariot beneath the stars and over the great, dark sea.

"Hello, Athena," the bright moon goddess greeted. "I wondered when you might come and say hello to me."

"I am sorry it has taken me so long."

"You are caring for a friend in need. That's important work."

Athena nodded as tears filled her eyes. Just a touch of sympathy and compassion from the goddess was all it took to open the floodgates, it seemed. "I have often admired you from afar."

"Likewise."

"I wonder if you've heard of Zeus's plans to introduce a female to the race of men."

"Indeed. She's called Pandora and is being delivered as a gift to Prometheus's brother now."

"His brother?"

"His twin, Epimetheus."

"Do you know where I can find him?"

"He lives in cave on an island in the East China Sea near his mother. Do you know the way?"

"Yes. Thank you, Selene."

"Take care, Athena."

As Athena flew from Selene's chariot, Aether appeared. "Prometheus is calling for you. He says it's urgent."

She followed the god of the upper air to Mount Ida, where Prometheus, wearing an agitated look on his face, said, "I had a terrible vision. Zeus gave my brother a jar and was told not to open it. But he opened it anyway, unleashing calamities beyond your wildest imaginings on the people below: disease, famine, sorrow, vice, greed, madness. It was terrible." He shuddered.

Athena's throat tightened as she exchanged worried glances with Clymene and Aether. "Which brother?"

"Epimetheus. You must go to him. Clymene can show you the way."

Athena followed the golden goddess across ocean and land to the East China Sea to the island where Clymene lived. In a cave not far from the one Prometheus and Athena had visited, they entered Epimetheus's abode. Athena was struck by the resemblance of the twin to his brother. Although he wore his hair and beard long, his basic features were eerily like those of Prometheus. His dark eyes lacked the unabashed kindness of his brother, however. They were jovial, perhaps, but not kind.

Pandora, the first female human, was already there dressed in the beautiful silver gown Athena had sewn. She held a clay jar in her hands.

Epimetheus noticed Athena and his mother immediately. "Hello. Have you come to meet my new wife? She's a gift from Zeus."

"We've come with an urgent message from your brother," Clymene explained. "He had a vision about that jar. You aren't to open it."

"Why would Zeus send me a wedding gift that wasn't meant to be opened?" Epimetheus said with a smirk. "My brother is clearly jealous of my bride and happiness."

Athena turned to Pandora. "Did Zeus give it to you?"

Pandora nodded. "He said it wasn't to be opened yet."

"Because he meant it for me," Epimetheus reasoned.

"Zeus is testing you," Athena said to the Titan. "Give it to me, and I will remove the temptation."

Pandora turned to Athena and was about to hand over the jar when Epimetheus grabbed it from her.

"Tell my brother that jealousy is understandable from someone in his situation," he said. "I'm sorry for him. I truly am. But what's mine is mine."

Before Athena and Clymene could intervene, Epimetheus pried open the lid.

CHAPTER EIGHT

Banished

S ince the opening of Pandora's jar, Athena's promise to Prometheus to protect their creations proved taxing. Like Clymene, Aether, and the Nephelae, she remained with him from sundown to sunup. But during most days, her duties called her away. One of her duties included helping Hephaestus to make more females. She worked tirelessly from morning until evening. Then, in the blink of an eye, Helios would begin his descent, and Athena would find herself rushing toward Crete to beat the eagle.

However, one day, twenty years after the first female had been created, after a huge victory over Poseidon for the patronage of one of the biggest thriving cities to have emerged in Greece, she took a day to celebrate this personal triumph, leaving the other gods to protect the people. She carried wine, cheese, and strawberries to Mount Ida— enough for all to share as she told her story.

"Poseidon and I agreed that the city would belong to whichever of us provided a gift most valued by the people," Athena began. "I gave the olive tree. Poseidon gave a river—though when he discovered that it was too salty to be of much use to them, he offered up horses."

"He gave horses to mortals to use as the gods do?" Aether asked.

"Yes," Athena replied. "It was an ingenious idea, I do admit. But I bested him again by offering them the bridles, reins, and chariots they would need to make use of the beasts."

"How very wise," one of the cloud nymphs praised. "I wouldn't have thought of that."

"The people were so pleased with me—and I so pleased by my victory—that I decided to institute an annual festival in honor of Prometheus." To her beloved she said, "You see, I don't want them to ever forget what you did for them, darling—the sacrifice you made." She turned back to the others. "The festival will include a torch relay commemorating the night he flew from village to village returning fire to them. The relay racers will pass though the potter and artisan district, where he's especially adored, and end at my altar on the Acropolis."

Athena smiled down at Prometheus, expecting him to return it; instead, his lips pressed into a thin line, and he refused to meet her gaze.

She fell on her knees beside him. "Are you not happy with my plans?"

"I thought you were wise, Athena," he muttered. "Do you wish to be chained to this rock beside me? How do you think your father will feel when he learns of this relay celebrating a treasonous act against him?"

Athena combed her fingers through his dark, curly hair. "Do not fear, my love. The people have forgotten how they lost the fire. Too many years have passed since that horrible night."

"Zeus has not forgotten," he insisted.

"It no longer concerns him," she assured him in a gentle voice. "He felt embarrassed and betrayed all those years ago, but he's moved on."

Prometheus abruptly rattled his chains, and Athena flinched with surprise.

"As long as he keeps me here," he bellowed, "he has not moved on!"

No one said a word for many minutes. Athena thought it best to remain silent, to avoid further agitating him.

Finally, in a calmer voice, he said, "My mother and Aether can come and go as they please. The Nephelae, too. But hence forward, I banish you from this rock, Athena."

Athena jumped to her feet. "No. I won't allow it. You can't banish me."

"The others have lived long lives and have accomplished great things," he continued. "But you have only just begun, and I am holding you back from your destiny."

"I am free to do as I wish," she insisted.

"At the cost of my happiness," he said gently. "It saddens me to see you here when you have so much to do elsewhere. It saddens me that you are nearly as much a prisoner as I."

His words reminded her of the many speeches her mother had made to her, urging her to leave their prison. She returned to her knees beside Prometheus and cupped his face. "My love, I can't bear to be away from you for long. Please don't ask this of me."

"Would you add to my pain?" he asked. "Is it not enough that the eagle comes for my liver every day?"

Athena felt the blood leave her face. "Don't I bring you some comfort?"

"You did for many years, and I thank you. But lately, when I look at you, I feel like I've chained you here, too. And the stories you share should comfort me, but they only make me long for the days when I was free."

"But—"

"Athena." His voice cracked as tears fell from his eyes. "I can no longer bear it. I've held my tongue for too long, and today, I am asking you to leave and to never return."

Tears now slipped from her eyes, too. "Do you not love me?"

"My answer will only hurt us both, so I will not give it."

Slowly, she returned to her feet, not knowing what else to say. The others avoided her gaze. She hoped they might say a word on her behalf.

No one did.

"Fine." She hadn't meant to speak in anger, but there it was. "I will go, though I truly believe in my heart that it will only add to your suffering. I await your apology on the day you come to your senses."

Without a word to the others, Athena flew away.

In need of love and support, she went directly to her temple in Athens, where her people adored her, but she was shocked by what she found. On her altar, Poseidon was passionately kissing a beautiful, young Athenian priestess named Medusa. Why were they here of all places? Wasn't anything sacred?

Full of jealousy and outrage, Athena cursed the priestess, turning her into a monster. Her pink, youthful skin transformed to a dull gray. Her bright, blue eyes became solid white. Her golden locks lifted in the wind and reshaped themselves into green snakes that hissed and curled around her head in a frenzied dance.

Athena growled, "From this day forward, any mortal who looks at you will instantly turn to stone. You will have no friend in the world, as I have none." To both lovers, she shouted, "Now, leave this place, and never return!"

Poseidon, his face nearly as white as the eye sockets of the monster, said nothing before he vanished.

The monster shrieked and slunk away. Athena heard her cries and wails until Medusa disappeared on the horizon.

It took many minutes for Athena to recover as she stood there panting near her altar. Once she regained control of her anger, she took her owl form and perched on a tree on the edge of the marketplace, where people were already talking about what had happened. There had been witnesses.

Athena was alarmed by rumors that her priestess had been innocent—that Poseidon had abused her. But Athena refused to believe them lest she turn into a monster, too.

Months later, when a princess from Lydia, famous for her tapestries, challenged her to a weaving contest, Athena gladly accepted the distraction. Thoughts of Prometheus and guilt over the curse she'd put on what might have been an innocent girl had been weighing on her and making her miserable. Even though she knew Prometheus could not hear her prayers because of the adamantine cuffs, she'd nevertheless been talking to him daily.

She needed to think about something else.

Although she believed the princess to be arrogant and emboldened to think she had a chance at besting a goddess, Athena thought it would be entertaining to humor her. She also believed it an ideal opportunity to show her people what they should strive for in their own handiwork.

It was decided that the theme for the tapestries would be the Olympian gods—a subject Athena was only too happy to depict. Having felt friendless since Prometheus banished her from his rock, she'd been looking for ways to become better acquainted with her family on Mount Olympus. Her recent conflict with Poseidon and her curse on the priestess hadn't helped matters. Only Hephaestus and Aphrodite seemed open to friendship with her. Everyone else seemed too busy to be bothered. Perhaps a fine tapestry showing them in a regal light would win them over.

She used the tapestry contest as an excuse to interview her fellow Olympians. Without exception, gods enjoyed talking about themselves, and Athena saw this as a way into their hearts.

Zeus proved a busy god, indeed. Much to Athena's chagrin, he spent an inordinate amount of time wooing the female humans, whom he'd come to call "women," which meant "of men." His infidelity enraged Hera, as it would any wife, and her disposition was almost constantly tainted by it. If Athena hadn't loved and been loved by her people, she would have regretted ever making them.

While Zeus could be benevolent and kind to them when he wished, he seemed to think of them as mere playthings. He seemed not to care about the impact his escapades had on their lives, not to mention the injury to Hera. However, Athena spent as much time as she could with him because it offered her opportunities to see her mother. She gazed into her father's eyes where her mother stood smiling, waving, and blowing kisses. She couldn't hear what her mother was saying, but she could understand the message. Metis was proud of her daughter and, even though she loved and missed her, was happy that she was free.

Athena found it easier to overlook her father's shortcomings because he could be likeable and even endearing when he was in the right mood. She was reminded of this when he approached her one day while she was having her breakfast in the garden behind the temple.

"It pleases me that you no longer remain by Prometheus's side," he began.

She had been about to explain that it had been Prometheus's choice, not hers, but Zeus continued, "I understood why you stayed with him. I understand the matters of the heart more than you might think. I did not begrudge you, even though Prometheus betrayed me, and I'm your father."

Athena climbed to her feet. "I—"

He lifted his palm to stop her. "That's water under the bridge. You are with me now, and that's what matters. And, I must say how proud I am of the work you are doing below."

She didn't know what to say, but fortunately he left before the silence between them became awkward.

Athena was pleased a few days into the weaving competition when Artemis invited her on a stag hunt in the Scottish mountains. Athena breathed in the crisp Scottish air, feeling invigorated by the rugged landscape that stretched before them. Pine trees towered over the rolling hills, their branches whispering in the wind. Not having used a bow, Athena gripped her spear, ready for action.

Artemis moved with the grace of a woodland nymph, her lithe form blending seamlessly into the wilderness. Her silver arrows gleamed in the dappled sunlight, a testament to her skill as the goddess of the hunt. Athena couldn't help but admire her sister's prowess, a flicker of rivalry igniting within her.

As they trekked deeper into the forest, the distant call of a stag echoed through the trees, stirring the air with anticipation. Athena felt her heart quicken with excitement, her senses sharpening as she focused on the hunt ahead. She glanced at Artemis, a silent understanding passing between them.

With stealth and determination, they tracked their quarry through the dense undergrowth, their footsteps light and sure. The forest seemed to come alive around them, every rustle of leaves and snap of twigs guiding them closer to their elusive prey.

Finally, they caught sight of the magnificent beast, its antlers reaching towards the sky in a proud display of strength. Athena felt a surge of admiration for the noble creature, a hint of regret tugging at her heart as she gripped her spear.

But there was no room for hesitation in the hunt, and with a steady hand, Artemis notched her bow and drew back the string, her eyes fixed on their target with unwavering focus.

Artemis released her arrow, the sound of its flight piercing the silence of the forest. For a heartbeat, the stag stood motionless against the backdrop of the undergrowth.

Then, with a mighty leap, it bounded into the depths of the forest. Athena and Artemis exchanged eager smiles before following the magnificent creature into the shadows. The thrill of the chase coursed through Athena as she ran behind her sister.

When the stag came into view, Athena launched her spear with strength and precision, bringing the beast to its knees. It staggered and fell into the lush undergrowth.

"We make a good team," Artemis said, sending a rush of joy through Athena's heart.

"Indeed. Shall we gift our kill to the nearest village?"

"I like the way you think."

On their way back to Mount Olympus, Artemis said, "Did you know they are calling us the virgin goddesses?"

"Who is calling us that?" Athena asked.

"The people. They seem to be aware of the affairs of the gods. You, me, and Hestia are known as the virgin goddesses."

"If Prometheus weren't bound to his rock, I doubt that would be true of me."

Artemis gave her a solemn nod. "I know how you feel. My love, Callisto, is trapped in the heavens as the constellation Ursa Major. If she were free, I would be no virgin."

"I wonder what Hestia's story is," Athena said as they reached the gates.

"She's too devoted to Zeus to take a lover. The people seem to think we three are virtuous for our virginity, but they are ignorant of our true struggles."

"Indeed. Thanks for sharing your hunt with me today."

The sister goddesses shook hands. Then Artemis commanded the gates of Mount Olympus to open, and she flew back to her rooms, leaving Athena behind.

At least she'd made some progress.

Later that week she found Apollo and Hermes in the Olympian palace making music with the Muses. Apollo played his lyre—which had been made by Hermes when the messenger god was still a babe—and

Hermes played his pipe. Wanting to join in the chorus, Athena quickly fashioned a wooden flute and began to harmonize with them. They were having a grand time, and she had just begun to feel like she fit in, when she caught a glimpse of her reflection in Hermes's shield. With her cheeks puffed out and her lips pursed, she looked ugly and distorted. Embarrassed, she tossed the flute from Mount Olympus and returned to her rooms to work on her tapestry alone.

When the time came to appear on the Acropolis of Athens to exhibit her tapestry alongside Princess Arachne from Lydia, Athena looked forward to the love and praise she had come to expect from her people. No matter how low she felt over the loss of Prometheus, the loss of her mother, and her trouble fitting in with the other Olympians, she could always count on her people to be there for her.

She and Arachne stood—each with her tapestry rolled in her arms—before the Parthenon, surrounded by gods and Athenians. Apollo shot a silver arrow into the air to signal that the contestants should unfurl their rolls.

Gasps filled the air. Then people began murmuring and laughing among themselves as they pointed to Arachne's tapestry. The gods paled. Zeus became red-faced and seemed ready to throw his lightning bolt. Athena, who had created a beautiful scene of the gods sitting on their thrones in the great hall was at first confused by the crowd's reaction. Then, she turned to study the tapestry of her competitor and was appalled. Although the weaving itself was high-quality and nearly as good as Athena's own, the subject was disrespectful to the gods. They were depicted in amorous positions, naked and undignified, like animals. Zeus was shown consorting with three women at once. Athena herself was depicted bare and kneeling in a passionate embrace with the shackled Prometheus as an eagle flew overhead.

Mortified, Athena tore the tapestry to shreds and commanded Arachne to return to Lydia and to never set foot in Athens again. Her people scattered, and the gods returned home.

Later that night, Athena flew to the Parthenon, intending to mount her tapestry on the wall behind her altar, when she found Arachne there hanging by a rope and, by all appearances, dead. Moved to pity, Athena loosened the rope and prayed to Hermes.

He appeared before she had breathed her next breath.

"Can I bring her back?" Athena asked. "Or have you taken her soul to the Underworld?"

"She's not dead yet but is too far gone to save."

Athena quickly turned the princess into a spider and the rope became a cobweb.

"I suppose that's one way to save her," the messenger god said before he flew away.

"There, there," Athena said to the princess. "You can still carry out your life's work. Be a weaver like no other."

Arachne said nothing—how could she? She was a spider. And Athena returned to her rooms.

Full of despair, Athena could not stay away from Prometheus a moment longer. A year had passed since that horrible day he had banished her from Mount Ida—the longest year of her life. She had to see him, to touch his face, to remind him of how much she loved him. And just as importantly, she needed to hear that he still loved her, too.

She waited for nightfall, when the eagle would have left and Prometheus would be unconscious, before making her appearance on the top of Mount Ida.

The cloud nymphs were reluctant to part and make way for her to pass, but she pressed through them.

"You shouldn't be here," Clymene insisted as she wiped the blood from her son's skin.

Aether, who was shooing away a vulture, glared at her with his chrome-colored eyes. "You'll only upset him. Go home to Mount Olympus."

Athena felt she did not have a home. For so long, her mother's presence was home to her. Soon after, the company of Prometheus became home. This past year, she felt like a transient being, a seed without roots blowing in the wind. She supposed the Parthenon had been the closest thing to home, but it had been tainted by Poseidon and Arachne.

"I want to see him," she said.

"You have. Now go," Clymene pleaded.

"I want him to lay eyes on me, too," she said.

"Selfish girl," Aether complained. "No good will come from this."

"I want him to know that I haven't forgotten him," Athena explained as tears welled in her eyes.

Clymene spoke through gritted teeth, "But that's precisely what he most desires."

Prometheus began to stir. His lids fluttered and then opened. Athena held her breath as his eyes found hers.

"Athena?" he said gently, as if he were still in the realm of dreams.

She fell on her knees beside him and cupped his face beneath the darkening sky. "How I've missed you." She kissed his forehead, his cheeks, his nose, his lips. "Oh, my darling."

"Stop." He recoiled from her. "Athena, stop!"

She sat up and stared at him with wide eyes. "Aren't you glad to see me?"

"I'm the opposite of glad. Please honor my wishes and leave."

She hated looking weak before the others, but she couldn't prevent the tears from spilling down her cheeks. Nor could she stop her limbs from trembling or her voice from shaking as she said, "You once swore on the River Styx to do everything in your power to help me."

"And you are making it difficult to keep that oath," he growled. "Now go and never return."

Athena wanted to throw herself at him and beg him to change his mind, to love her again, to be tender towards her. She wanted him to stroke her cheek, tuck a strand of hair behind her ear, and gaze longingly into her eyes. She wanted anything but this cold, hard, angry god commanding her to leave.

But wanting it did not make it so.

She noticed Selene overhead gazing down at her from her silver chariot. How many others were watching her, wondering what she would do?

Without saying another word, she flew to her temple in Athens where it was dark and quiet. The city was asleep, or nearly so, and she was alone. She curled in a corner, hugged her legs, bowed her head, and wept. She wept for her mother. She wept for Prometheus. She wept for the goddess she wished she could be. And she wept for the monster, Medusa, and the spider, Arachne.

After a long, hard, body-wrenching cry, she wiped her eyes, straightened her back, and gritted her teeth. She resolved never to weep again for what was lost. Instead, she would pour her energy into leading the people she had helped to create. She would turn men into heroes.

CHAPTER NINE

Heroes and Monsters

A thena sat on her throne polishing a shield given to her by Hephaestus. Zeus and Hera were visiting the garden of the Hesperides, Hestia was in her kitchen, and Artemis and Apollo had gone hunting. As usual, Poseidon and Hades were in their palaces in the sea and Underworld respectively, and Hephaestus was in his forge. Because Demeter, Persephone, and Hecate had gone fishing, only Ares, Aphrodite, and the Charities shared the great hall with Athena, until Hermes appeared at her side.

"I have news and need a favor," the messenger god said.

"I'm listening."

Hermes tugged at his short, curly beard. "A man named Perseus hailing from Serifos has got himself into a bit of trouble."

"How so?"

"You see, the king is enamored with Perseus's mother but knows the son disapproves. So, the king attempted to bring dishonor to the son by hosting a banquet and asking his guests to bring gifts of horses, knowing Perseus doesn't have one."

"Finding him one should be easy enough."

"There's more," Hermes explained. "Perseus wanted to avoid looking foolish by instead offering to bring the king anything he wanted in place of a horse, and—this is where things get really bad—the king asked for the head of Medusa."

Aphrodite and Ares looked up from whatever they were doing, their curiosity piqued.

"What will you do?" Aphrodite asked her.

Athena turned to Hermes. "What did you have in mind?"

"Medusa is a lonely thing, Athena. She's a hermit, not wanting to bring harm to others. It's a horrible life you've cursed her with."

Hermes wasn't telling Athena anything she didn't already know, and his saying it out loud to her face and before the others angered her. She bit down the rage and asked, "Again I ask, what do you have in mind?"

"I've already given the boy my winged sandals and sickle and was hoping you'd loan him your shield."

"This shield? This new shield I just received from Hephaestus?"

Hermes cleared his throat. "It reflects like a mirror better than mine and will help Perseus avoid looking directly at the monster."

Athena wasn't sure what to say. Medusa didn't deserve death, but perhaps Hermes was right in suggesting that it would be a mercy to kill her.

"Perseus will need our guidance," she finally said.

Hermes clapped his hands, grabbed her cheeks, and smacked a kiss on her lips.

She wasn't sure whether to be offended or amused by the kiss but finally settled on the latter.

"Listen to me," she continued. "This could go very badly for the boy. The head of Medusa, even severed, will petrify any mortal who looks at it. We must be smart about this." Then, she added, "And if Perseus succeeds, the head is mine."

"I'm never anything but smart, I assure you," Hermes said in a teasing tone. "And I couldn't care less about who keeps the head."

"Where is Perseus now?"

"He's waiting for us on a ship in the Aegean Sea not far from Serifos. I was hoping you would know where to find Medusa's cave."

"No, but I know who does. Let's go."

As they flew together from Mount Olympus, Athena wondered about the kiss. Had it been a brotherly one? Or had she picked up on a different feeling? She'd been reminded once by Apollo that although humans live according to the rule that siblings must not marry, that had never been true for the gods. Zeus and Hera were perfect examples.

Hermes's resemblance to Prometheus had not gone unnoticed by Athena. His dark, curly hair, short beard, and dark eyes—and even his physique—would make it easy to mistake him for the Titan from afar. Aside from a slightly longer nose and higher cheekbones, only the mood of the eyes and the smile set him apart. Whereas Prometheus's eyes were kind and his smile warm, Hermes's were taunting and playful.

Athena was bothered by the fact that she'd enjoyed the kiss.

When they reached Perseus's ship, Athena worried that she was getting more trouble than she had bargained for. Perseus had already exposed his foolishness in his rash offer to bring the king *anything*, and now he was sailing aimlessly in the Aegean with no clue to Medusa's whereabouts.

She followed Hermes to the deck of the ship beneath the billowing sails. Perseus stood behind the wheel looking as though he had swallowed a frog. Three of his crew were coiling ropes near the stern.

The boy, noticing the gods, went down on his knees. "Thank you for coming to my aid. My fate is in your hands."

Athena decided she liked Perseus. She could sense that he had a good heart. The reason he was in this mess was because he had wanted to protect his mother. Yes, he had been rash in his attempt to save face, but the king had behaved cruelly. Athena wanted to help Perseus. She wanted him to become a hero.

"You need to set your sails for Swan Island in the Ionian Sea, not far from the castle of Phorcys and Keto," Athena commanded.

The boy climbed to his feet and barked orders to his crew, who quickly changed the ship's course Then, Perseus asked, "Does Medusa live there?"

"No," Athena replied. "But the Gray Sisters do, and that's whom we're going to see first."

Hermes gave Athena a wink and said to her telepathically, *The Gray Sisters, huh? We're on an exciting adventure together, are we not? I look forward to seeing how it all ends for us.*

Athena had learned about the Gray Sisters from her mother. The three triplets were born with gray hair and hag-like features, and they shared one eye and one tooth. They had the gift of foreknowledge and were often sought by gods and mortals for hints of future events. But their island was heavily guarded by their parents, Phorcys and Keto, monsters who lived in an ancient castle at the bottom of the Ionian Sea.

"We'll need a diversion to get past the Old Man of the Sea and his crusty wife," Athena said to Hermes, referring to the Gray Sisters' parents. "Can you come up with something?"

"Why, Athena, diversions are my specialty," he said with a teasing smile and a gleam in his eyes. "I know just the thing for our crusty couple."

When the ship neared Swan Island, Hermes flew above the location of the ancient underwater castle and began to play his pipe. Soon, fish of every kind were leaping into the air in a strange kind of dance to his tune. Not long into this fish dance, Phorcys and Keto emerged at the water's surface with hungry eyes. Phorcys—a giant who was half man and half lobster—snapped with claws and mouth, doing triple duty unlike his mermaid wife. While they chased the fish and filled their bellies, Athena directed the ship to Swan Island and to the Gray Sisters.

Perseus anchored the ship as close to the island as he dared and, using the winged sandals from Hermes, followed Athena to the island.

"The Gray Sisters won't give up Medusa's location willingly," Athena warned the young man.

"Do you have a strategy in mind?" Perseus asked as he flailed his arms in the air, unused to flight.

"Indeed. Don't even mention Medusa until you have their eye."

"What?"

"Ask about your future. They'll pass the eye from one sister to the next to pull their collective visions. That's when you reach out and grab it and refuse to return it until they've disclosed Medusa's whereabouts."

"Shouldn't you be the one to take the eye?" he wondered.

"My presence will only upset them. I'll be hiding outside the cave."

"Will you intervene if they make an attempt on my life, goddess?"

Athena could hear the fear in the boy's voice. He hadn't intended to become a hero. He'd only meant to protect his mother.

"Indeed," she said. "You have my power behind you, Perseus. You can do this."

Moments later, Perseus emerged from the cave, screaming. Athena grabbed his arms and returned him to the ship, where Hermes was already waiting.

"Keto and Phorcys are on their way," Hermes warned. "We've pulled up the anchor. Which way do we sail?"

Athena turned to the trembling Perseus. "Did you learn Medusa's location?"

With quivering lips, the young man replied, "The island of Sarpedon."

"That's near Cypress," Hermes said. "Order your men to sail east."

Perseus snapped out of his terror and barked to his men, "Hoist the sails! Turn our course due east to Cypress!"

Just then, the old crab-man leapt from the sea and was about to land on the bow of the ship when Athena flung her spear into his belly and knocked him back. Then, not wanting to lose her prized weapon made for her by her mother, she flew to the beast as he was about to submerge, and she pried it from him before returning to the deck of the ship.

Hermes looked at her with wide eyes, clearly impressed. "Damn."

Athena removed her crested helmet and returned Hermes's grin.

His admiration pleased her more than she cared to admit—to him or to herself.

The adventure with Hermes and Perseus filled Athena with new life, but the view of Crete on their way to Cypress sobered her. There on the peak of Mount Ida was her beloved chained to his rock and awaiting the eagle. The Nephelae noticed her as she passed on the ship, and they gazed down at her mournfully, raining tears into the sea and filling Athena with guilt. How could she enjoy a thrilling adventure while the love of her life was suffering?

Feeling somber now, Athena thought of Medusa and the trauma they were about to inflict on her. The quicker Perseus took her head, the better. As they anchored about fifty yards from Sarpedon, she turned to the young man. "I will be with you every step of the way, but you won't be able to see me. I don't want Medusa to be alarmed by my presence. Use my shield to get close to her, raise the sickle, and swing—all the while trusting that I will guide the blade."

"Yes, goddess. Thank you, goddess."

The poor boy was trembling with fear. Guiding the blade in his shaky hands would be a challenge. Nevertheless, they entered the cave together—Athena invisible to mortal eyes—and crept inside Medusa's lair.

The monster was sleeping on a cot along the furthest wall near a cozy fire, but they hadn't yet traversed even half the length of the cave before she snapped upright, her serpent hair alert and hissing, and her white eyes wide with fear and rage.

"Who dares to enter my cave?" she screeched. "Look into my eyes and identify yourself!"

Perseus resisted the temptation to face her by studying her reflection in the shield. The reflection danced with the light from the fire, making it difficult for the boy to gauge the monster's true position.

Athena wanted to encourage Perseus to move more quickly and to trust that she would help, but she couldn't risk being heard by Medusa. She was surprised, however, when the boy made a sudden move to attack. Athena rushed to the blade and helped it meet its mark.

When the deed was done, Athena mourned, ashamed of what she had done to Medusa. She was so distracted by her thoughts that she failed to notice Perseus leaving the cave with the head, the snake hair still violently squirming.

"Perseus, wait!" she cried. "The bag!"

Before she could stop him—for the sandals of Hermes were swift—Perseus flew toward his home of Serifos. On the way, he noticed a princess perched on a rock being attacked by a terrible beast.

"Princess Andromeda, it's me, Perseus. Close your eyes!" he shouted to the beautiful girl. "And do not open them until I say!"

The princess covered her face just as Perseus swooped down and revealed Medusa's head to the beast, immediately turning it into a rock that became a permanent part of the island.

Athena was thoroughly impressed. The boy had indeed become a hero.

"Keep your eyes closed," Perseus said to Andromeda. "I'm going to take you to safety, but you'll have to trust me. Climb onto my back."

The girl circled her arms around his neck and her legs around his waist, and, with eyes closed, burrowed her face in the back of his neck. Athena followed them to Serifos.

When he reached his island home, he hovered in the air with the head hidden from view and shouted a warning to the people below, who had gathered to gawk at the spectacle of him in the winged sandals of Hermes. "What I have is for the king's eyes only!"

The people obediently covered their eyes, while the king looked up with curiosity. As Perseus lifted the head of Medusa, the king turned to stone. Then, Perseus stuffed the monster's head into the bag Athena had given him and turned to the princess.

"You can open your eyes."

The princess glanced around with lifted brows and wonderment on her face, clearly relieved to be free of the beast. "Thank you for rescuing me, Perseus. I thought that was the end for me."

"I'm the new king of Serifos. Marry me and become my queen?"

The princess nodded shyly.

Hermes caught up to Athena where she was watching the scene unfold. "A happy ending, wouldn't you say?"

She returned his playful smile. "Indeed, but what about his ship?"

"I instructed the crew to bring it to port. It's on its way as we speak."

Athena turned and saw the billowing sails as the ship changed its course to Serifos. "I'd say that was a job well done."

As they flew toward Mount Olympus—Hermes with his sandals and sickle and Athena with her shield and bag—Hermes pointed to the island where Perseus had petrified the beast attacking Andromeda.

"When Medusa's blood dripped below, the babes she'd been carrying inside of her made their escape."

"Poseidon's babes?" Athena asked.

"Yes. There they are. Queer little fellas, aren't they?"

Both were tiny and cute. One was a winged horse as white as snow. The other was a two-headed serpent, green as grass and blowing puffs of smoke in the air.

"You take the horse, and I'll take the serpent," Athena suggested.

With their things strapped to their backs and belts, they each swept up a creature.

"I'm in love," Athena said of the little beast in her arms. "I shall name her Amphisbaena."

"How can you tell it's a 'she?'"

"I can't, really. I suppose since there are two heads, they're a 'they.'" Athena laughed.

"This one's a cutie, too," Hermes said with a chuckle. "I'll let Zeus pick out a name for him."

"There's a cave beneath my temple that will make the perfect home for Amphisbaena."

"This little guy will have a stable on Mount Olympus, won't you boy?"

Full of good cheer, the two gods flew with their adopted babes back toward the mainland. Athena was so distracted by her new love that she failed to notice the island of Crete as she passed.

CHAPTER TEN

Amphisbaena and Pegasus

Athena sat on a rock in a cave beneath the Acropolis of Athens feeding ants to the baby Amphisbaena. The snake with a head on each end had grown in the few months since its birth to two feet long and three inches thick. Athena had been delighted to learn that it breathed fire, and with the little puffs of smoke that remained after each little spit, Amphisbaena could be taught to spell simple words.

Athena had come to call one end of the snake, "One," and the other end, "Two." When Athena got confused as to which head was which, Amphisbaena puffed out her little streams of fire, and the smoke behind spelled, "I am One," and "I am Two," near the corresponding head.

After all the ants had been eaten, Athena decided to take Amphisbaena swimming at a remote spring on the side of Mount Kithairon. It was a hot summer's day, and the spring was refreshing. The baby Amphisbaena loved the water as much as Athena did. They floated together on their backs and then after a while, turned and swam on their bellies, basking in the warmth of Helios.

"Hello, Athena," Hermes greeted from where he hovered above them beside the white, winged horse, which had come to be called Pegasus.

The baby Pegasus had grown to about three feet in length and two feet high.

"Hello, that's an impressive wingspan," Athena noted of the feathered wings that stretched at least four feet on either side. "What are you two doing here?"

"I saw you fly past us and, out of curiosity, came to see where you were going. Enjoying a nice dip in the stream, Amphisbaena?"

The little creature puffed up its snout on each end, spit small balls of fire, and in the smoke left behind, spelled, "One says yes," and "Two says yes."

"Well, lookie there," Hermes said with a laugh. "How clever is that?"

"You're welcome to join us," Athena offered. "The water feels delightful."

"I don't know about mixing horses and snakes. You should know better than that. They're natural enemies."

"But they're siblings."

Hermes turned to Pegasus. "What do you think? Should we go for a dip, too?"

The little horse nodded its head and swooped down into the stream beside Amphisbaena, who filled her mouths with water and playfully spit it out, creating arcs for Pegasus to swim and fly over and under. They entertained themselves for half an hour while Hermes joined Athena in the water to watch the magical creatures play. The two gods floated on their backs and laughed at the adorable babes.

"Now, that's entertainment," Hermes said after the creatures had calmed down.

"I think they've worn themselves out."

Amphisbaena curled on top of a rock in the middle of the stream to sunbathe. Pegasus climbed on the rock beside her, shook the water from his coat and wings, and then lay on his belly and closed his eyes.

"Look, they're fast friends," Athena pointed out.

"For now," Hermes said. "But let's see how they are together when they're fully grown."

Athena and Hermes climbed onto the bank and stretched out to sunbathe, too, allowing the rays of Helios to dry them off.

After a while, Hermes asked, "You haven't stolen my winged sandals, have you?"

"Why would you suspect me of that?" Athena asked, taken aback.

"Oh, don't be offended. I take things that don't belong to me all the time."

"Maybe no one stole them. Maybe you've misplaced them. Where did you last see them?"

"I don't remember where I put them after I retrieved them from Perseus."

Amphisbaena suddenly lifted her heads and spit out balls of fire. In the smoke left behind, she wrote, "One says stables," and "Two says stables."

"What are you trying to tell me, Amphisbaena?" Athena asked.

The little creature spit fire again and in the smoke spelled, "Sandals."

Athena and Hermes exchanged looks of wonder.

"Does your little snake have a gift?" Hermes asked.

"There's only one way to find out." Athena climbed to her feet. "Come on, little babes!" she said to the playmates. "Let's go together to the stables on Mount Olympus and see if Hermes's winged sandals are there."

Since Amphisbaena couldn't fly, Athena and Hermes draped her across the back of Pegasus, and together they flew north from Mount Kithairon to Mount Olympus. Amphisbaena seemed frightened at first, but once she saw that she was in no danger, she began to enjoy the ride, spitting little balls of fire along the way that left phrases like, "One says fun," and "Two says beauty" in her wake.

Athena glanced over the landscape below and said, "Indeed, it's very beautiful. I sometimes forget to take notice."

After commanding the gates to let them in, the foursome flew directly to the stables. The four winds weren't at home—they were probably charioting Zeus around. But Ares and Apollo's horses were in their stalls eating hay. Amphisbaena slithered from the back of Pegasus, causing the other horses to protest with skittish grunts and snorts.

"Settle down," Hermes commanded. "She's not going to hurt you."

Amphisbaena slithered past the horses to the final stall.

"That's where I keep Pegasus," Hermes pointed out. "Surely I would have noticed my sandals if I'd left them in there."

Amphisbaena burrowed into the hay and pulled up a winged sandal with her teeth.

"Good girl!" Athena praised.

"Well, lookie there," Hermes said with astonishment. "They were buried in the hay the whole time."

"I'm happy to accept your apology," Athena teased. "Along with your thanks."

"You have both, my dear." Hermes dug the second sandal from the hay, and all four of them laughed.

Within a year, Amphisbaena grew from two to twelve feet in length and to at least a foot thick. Each of her heads was the size of a goat, and they'd taken on more dragon-like features with pronounced snouts, rows of teeth, long, pointed tongues, and fire-spans of twenty feet. Although she was mostly obedient to Athena, she'd become less docile and playful and somewhat resentful of what she'd come to consider less of a home and more of a prison.

Athena tried to get her out at least once a month, but it was far more difficult to take her places now that she was fully grown. Today, Athena offered to take her to their favorite stream on Mount Kithairon, where they'd spent many days the summer before swimming with Hermes and Pegasus. Amphisbaena perked up. She loved to swim and to bask in the sun.

Amphisbaena fed on fish as she slithered in the refreshing stream beside Athena. Each head took in mouthfuls of water and spit them in the air, creating arcs of waterfalls for Athena to swim under and fly over, just as she had done for Pegasus a year ago. After a while, they sunbathed together on a rock and fell asleep.

"Hello, Athena, I thought I'd find you here," Hermes called from above.

Athena opened her eyes to find Hermes astride Pegasus in the bright, blue sky. The winged horse was fully grown at eight feet from head to back hoof and a wingspan of at least eight feet on either side.

Before Athena could reply, Amphisbaena lifted her heads, her body forming a "U."

Pegasus, not having seen his old playmate for many months, shrieked and reared back, knocking Hermes off before flying away.

Amphisbaena looked mournfully at Athena before spitting a ball of fire and spelling, "What did I do?"

"It's not your fault, Amphisbaena," Hermes said as he landed on the rock beside them. "Horses and snakes just don't get along."

Amphisbaena did not seem to like what the messenger god had to say, for she lifted both heads and shot fire into the sky for five long seconds. The words left behind in the smoke said, "What a coward."

Athena and Hermes laughed.

"Maybe we can get him to come around," Athena suggested. "Come on, Hermes. Amphisbaena gets bored easily these days. Can't you convince Pegasus to be her friend?"

Just then, they heard a loud shriek echoing off the gulf to the west. Athena darted into the sky above Mount Kithairon with Hermes close behind her.

"It's Pegasus," Hermes said, just before he took off.

Amphisbaena looked up at Athena with alarm. Athena pointed to where the half-lobster, half-man and father of the sea monsters had trapped one of Pegasus's hooves in his pincher. Pegasus frantically flapped his wings and kicked with his one free back hoof to escape but to no avail. Amphisbaena leapt from the mountainside into the air and soared toward the sea. Athena quickly followed.

"You can't fly! What are you doing?"

Her serpent dragon dove into the gulf about a hundred yards from the monster and swam at lightning speed in its direction. She soon coiled herself around the monster's head, suffocating him until he had no choice but to release Pegasus and return to the depths of the sea.

"Way to go, Amphisbaena!" Hermes shouted with glee.

Athena grinned when Pegasus swooped down and nudged the serpent dragon onto his back. Athena and Hermes happily followed as Pegasus flew with Amphisbaena on his back all the way to her cave in Athens.

Heracles

Athena continued to distract herself over the years by caring for Amphisbaena, overseeing her city, and helping men to become heroes. She taught Bellerophon of Corinth to bridle and ride Pegasus. She showed Theseus of Athens how to defeat the Minotaur and save the lives of countless Athenian youth. More recently, a descendant of Perseus by the name of Heracles, or sometimes Hercules, the son of Zeus and the mortal Alcmene, had caught Athena's attention.

She'd helped him once, after his birth, by tricking Hera into nursing him. Athena had steered clear of him ever since, not wanting to incur Hera's wrath, who hated the reminder of her husband's infidelity. However, after Hera drove Heracles to kill his wife and children, Athena felt sorry for him, especially when, horrified by what he had done to his family, he visited the Oracle at Delphi to see what he might do to atone for his crimes. Unbeknownst to him, Hera was there guiding the Oracle, who proclaimed that he must serve King Eurystheus for ten years and do whatever the king required.

Athena spent the next ten years helping Heracles undergo ten labors assigned by the king. Heracles defeated the Nemean lion with his bare hands. He slayed the Hydra. He captured the golden hind that was sacred to Artemis. He caught the Erymanthian boar. He cleaned the Augean Stables, the home of 3,000 cattle with poisonous feces. Using a rattle Athena had given him, he scared the man-eating Stymphalian birds and shot them down with his bow and arrows as they attempted to fly away. He captured the Cretan bull. He stole the flesh-eating mares of Diomedes, retrieved the girdle of Hippolyta, and obtained the cattle of the monster Geryon.

Heracles had been promised immortality after completing these ten labors, but the king tricked him into agreeing to two more. Fearing the hero would despair, Athena flew down and revealed herself to him.

They were in Africa near the Atlas Mountains. Above them on the highest peak, Prometheus's brother continued to hold the sky on his shoulders.

Heracles fell to his knees at the sight of Athena. "Goddess! I owe so much to you! And now you honor me with your presence!"

"I'm sorry that your labors have been extended. I promise to help you in any way that I can."

"Oh, thank you, goddess!" He climbed to his feet. "I've been ordered to steal golden apples from the garden of the Hesperides. It's guarded by the one-hundred-headed serpent, Ladon, and the three Hesperides. It's not far from here, but I can't think of a strategy. Any advice?"

Athena wished she knew what to say. Even if she helped to guide his arrows, fighting one hundred heads was risky, not to mention doing so while avoiding the Hesperides—the three nymphs who also guarded the golden apple tree. Remembering that the nymphs were the daughters of Atlas, and that Atlas was the brother of Prometheus, Athena got an idea.

She hadn't allowed herself to think of him for so many years. It had been forty since that first terrible night and twenty since he'd banished her. The thought of seeing him filled her with a mixture of emotions. Foremost, she wondered if she was making an excuse to see him. Was it for Heracles or for herself that she wanted to advise the hero to question the Titan?

Her time with Prometheus seemed like another life altogether, or like a dream that sometimes felt real and sometimes didn't. It was hard to believe there was a time when he was free, a time when they could lie in one another's arms and smile and touch and kiss. A time when they spoke tenderly to one another and laughed and danced. Had any of it ever happened?

Suddenly, Athena lifted her chin. A second idea had followed the first, and this one had her head spinning.

"Are you sure about this?" Heracles asked her as they climbed Mount Ida together. "The other deities will let me pass?"

"Once they hear your offer, they'll do anything you ask," Athena assured him.

As they neared the peak, she was surprised to find Aether and the Nephelae gone. Only Clymene remained by her son's side, even though it was nearly sundown. Where had the others gone?

Prometheus noticed Athena and sat up with alarm. "Has something happened?"

It saddened her to realize that he could imagine no other scenario for her visit than a tragic one. As much as she wanted to fly to him, to cup his face, and to press her lips to his, she felt awkward, nervous, and afraid. Her heart quivered, as did her hands, which she hid behind her back.

"This is Heracles, also known as Hercules. He's a mortal son of Zeus," Athena introduced. "Heracles, this is Prometheus and his mother, Clymene."

Heracles went down on one knee. "It's a great honor to meet you. I've come with an offer."

"What kind of offer?" Clymene asked.

"I've been tasked by gods and my king with collecting golden apples from the garden of the Hesperides, but I have no idea how to proceed. In exchange for advice, I'll kill the eagle when it comes, and set you free."

Clymene gasped.

Prometheus's mouth dropped open as he searched Athena's face. "But Zeus—"

"Forbade the gods from interfering," Athena said. "He never forbade mortals."

Clymene burst into tears of joy. "Oh, my son. Free at last!"

"Free from the eagle, but not from these chains," Prometheus pointed out. "But I shall be glad of it, nevertheless. I'd rather be miserable from boredom than pain."

Heracles showed him the key. "My father gave it to me. He wants to exalt me after what Hera has put me through."

Clymene shouted with joy, "At last! At last!"

Though his eyes widened with surprise, Prometheus said, "I dare not hope. I can't bear the thought of being disappointed. I don't trust Zeus."

"To show you that I mean what I say," Heracles began, "I shall kill the eagle and free you from your chains before seeking your advice."

"I will help you regardless of the outcome," Prometheus promised.

"You may not have faith in me," Heracles said. "But I have enough for us both."

"Where have the others gone?" Athena asked Clymene.

The golden goddess frowned. "It became too much for them to bear."

Prometheus steeled himself as Helios made his descent. Athena's heart raced when she saw the bird on the horizon. She'd forgotten how horrible it was—the anxiety just before the eagle came.

Heracles got several shots off in a row, striking the eagle in the breast and in both eyes with his arrows. The shrieks from the eagle echoed on the mountainside as it fell to its death. Heracles then promptly released Prometheus from the adamantine chains.

The Titan, not having stood in forty years, struggled to his feet with the help of his mother.

Again, Athena felt trapped between the desire to go to him and the fear of being rejected by him. What if he no longer loved her?

"Listen to me, Heracles," Prometheus said with tears slipping down his face. "Go to my brother Atlas and offer to give him a break from holding up the sky if he will swear on the River Styx to bring you a barrel of golden apples from Hera's tree."

"I will do it!" Heracles cried.

"But wait," Prometheus warned. "He will want to deliver the apples himself and leave you there with the sky. So, here's what you do: When he returns with the apples and offers to take them to the king, ask him if he'll just take the sky for a moment while you pad your shoulders. Knowing my brother, he'll fall for it. Once the sky is safely in his hands, take the apples and run."

"Thank you, my lord," Heracles said gratefully. "I will do as you say."

"I must go and help him," Athena said, wishing Prometheus would take her into his arms, or show her any sign of affection, any sign that he still cared.

"Of course, you must," he agreed.

"Oh, Prometheus," she said as she turned to go. "I'm so happy to see you free. I never thought this day would come."

With joy in her heart, Athena followed Heracles down the mountainside to his ship, where they sailed toward Africa and the garden of the Hesperides.

It took two days for Heracles to reach the highest peak of the Atlas Mountains—even with Athena blowing into the sails to speed up the ship—and another day for him to bargain with Atlas, receive the golden apples, and trick Atlas into taking back the sky. With the labor complete, Athena turned her attention to finding Prometheus.

While she'd been watching over Heracles, she'd been pondering what to say to Prometheus when she next saw him. Should she protect her heart by waiting for him to reveal his feelings to her? Did he still love her? Or had his feelings for her faded? What if he never revealed them? What if they each held back, waiting for the other to make a move, and were left in a stalemate?

No, she decided it would be far better to confess her love to him and be broken-hearted than to risk never knowing his true feelings—especially when there was a possibility that he still loved her as deeply as she loved him.

Excited and nervous, Athena hastened to Mount Olympus. Finding no sign of Prometheus there, she flew to the East China Sea, hoping to find him in his cave near his mother. His brother, Epimetheus, had been thrown into the Titan pit after opening Pandora's jar, so when she didn't find Prometheus in his own cave, she went to his twin's. There, she found a den of snakes and nothing more. She god-traveled to the mouth of Clymene's cave.

"Prometheus?" she called.

The golden goddess appeared. "He's not here."

"Hello, Clymene. I'm so happy to see you anywhere else but Mount Ida. Isn't it nice to be home?"

"Indeed, though I miss my children."

"At least you still have Prometheus," Athena said gently.

"Do I?"

Athena's heart stopped in her chest. Had Zeus betrayed her and thrown Prometheus into the Titan pit? Or had he done something worse? "Where is he, Clymene?"

The goddess shrugged. "He wouldn't tell me where he was going."

"Why not?" Athena's heart began to race.

"He doesn't trust your father. He's gone into hiding and wouldn't jeopardize me or my freedom by telling me where. He wants us to be safe, Athena."

Athena dropped to her knees. She'd never felt so dizzy, so weak, or so nearly close to fainting.

Clymene brought her fresh water to drink.

"Thank you." After taking a few sips, Athena said, "If you see him again, please tell him that it's my choice to make—whether to jeopardize my freedom—not his."

"I don't expect to see him."

"But if you do."

"Athena, move on with your life. Let the past be the past."

She clenched her fists. "Again, it's my choice to make."

"If I see him, I will tell him."

Once Athena had left the cave, she searched every inch of the earth for Prometheus as she prayed, *If you ever loved me, come to me.* After scouring the land and all its crevices, she searched the seven seas, examining every dolphin she passed. When she found no sign of her beloved, she began again.

CHAPTER TWELVE

The Caduceus

Dressed in her finest golden gown and cloak, Athena rode with Hephaestus and Aphrodite to a wedding feast Zeus was hosting on Mount Pelion in honor of Thetis—the sea nymph that had raised Hephaestus after Hera had flung him from Mount Olympus—and Peleus, the king of Phthia. Her eyes scanned the landscape below for Prometheus, as they always did. She'd been doing it for over a year while she'd helped Jason and the Argonauts search for the golden fleece and attempt to regain his rightful place as King of Thessaly, but nothing had gone as planned.

"You know why Zeus is hosting the wedding party, don't you?" Aphrodite asked her companions.

Athena knew but didn't reply. She was searching for Prometheus.

"No, why?" Hephaestus asked from behind the reins.

"Prometheus once told him that a son of Thetis would be greater than his father. Zeus had been courting Thetis at the time and has been trying to marry her off to a mortal ever since they were created."

"I heard Thetis didn't want to marry," Hephaestus chimed in. "Not even Peleus, but he somehow persuaded her."

Hephaestus parked the chariot on the mountainside near Chiron's cave under a canopy of trees where many deities and royal subjects had already gathered at long banquet tables full of wine, bread, cheese, and roasted lamb and were listening to the Muses sing. Some of the attendees were dancing, too, including Chiron, the most noble of the Centaurs and a trainer of heroes.

As Athena was about to step from the chariot to join the others, Hermes offered her his hand and helped her down.

"You look beautiful," he said. "I hope you won't offend the bride."

Athena blushed and shook her head.

On the way to the table, Hermes twirled her under his arm and danced with her the rest of the way, making her giggle. She appreciated how he could distract her and make her smile even when all seemed lost. He pulled out a chair for her next to his and poured her a glass of wine. Aphrodite and Hephaestus joined them.

When the Muses finished their song, Peleus stood where he had been sitting by his bride and raised his golden goblet. "Many thanks to Lord Zeus for honoring us with this feast and to the great gods and goddesses for joining us in our celebration. Although your company is a treasured gift, we are also grateful for the other gifts you've given us. The god Apollo and the Muses have provided our entertainment. I understand the goddess Artemis was responsible for hunting the lamb and the goddess Hestia for roasting it. From Chiron, I received an ashen spear that I'm told was polished by the goddess Athena and forged by the god Hephaestus. Athena also gave us a beautifully handcrafted flute. From the goddess Aphrodite, we received a golden bowl. From the goddess Hera we received a fine silk cloak. My father-in-law Nereus gave us a basket of divine salt, and Lord Zeus, in addition to this feast, bestowed us with the wings of Arke. Please raise your glasses and drink a toast to the divine deities and their generosity."

As the wedding party raised their glasses and cried, "To the gods!" a winged deity flew into their midst and dropped something on the ground. Athena recognized Eris, who hadn't been invited because, as the goddess of discord, she usually caused problems. After dropping what must have been a gift, she flew away.

Swift Hermes was the first to reach the object. "It's a golden apple with a note. It reads 'To the fairest.'" He turned to Athena. "It must be for you."

Before Athena could take the apple, Hera flew over and intercepted it. "This apple is mine. It's from my tree, given to me by Gaia and guarded by Ladon and the Hesperides. I don't know how Eris stole it, but she did, and it isn't hers to give."

"But it says, 'To the fairest,'" Hephaestus argued. "Everyone knows that the fairest one among us is Aphrodite."

"Lord Zeus, you decide," Aphrodite said to her father. "To whom does this apple belong?"

Athena could tell that he did not want to answer. No matter whom he chose, he would incur the bitterness of the others.

"There's a shepherd on Mount Ida who recently awarded a contest to Ares and was quite fair about it," Zeus said. "I command Hermes to escort you three goddesses there and ask Paris to decide."

The last thing Athena wanted was to go to Mount Ida where Prometheus had been chained to his rock; but, before she could refuse, Hermes took her by the hand and led her and the other two goddesses from the wedding party. She decided not to object and flew with them across the sea to Crete, where they scoured the mountainside for the shepherd.

To Athena's annoyance, the shepherd and his goats weren't far from the mountain peak. No sign remained that Prometheus and his chains had ever been there, but the memories were seared into Athena's brain, and she could still see her beloved anxiously awaiting his punishment. On trembling legs, she followed Hermes and the other goddesses to the tree stump where Paris was sitting and eating, of all things, an apple.

Startled by the arrival of the gods, Paris jumped to his feet and then fell to his knees. "I am honored by your visit," he said with his head bowed.

Hermes quickly handed the golden apple to Paris and explained why they were there. As he did, Athena glanced up the hill. Helios had not yet begun to descend, but it wouldn't be long, and here she was competing in a beauty contest where her beloved had once been tortured. She felt the blood leave her face as she averted her eyes.

When Hermes had finished explaining, Paris returned to his tree stump and looked over the goddesses.

"You are all beautiful," he said wisely. "I don't know whom to choose."

"I'll give you great power as the king of Eurasia if you choose me," Hera said suddenly.

Aphrodite bent over Paris, mussed his hair, and said, "I'll give you great love with the most beautiful woman in the world—Helen of Troy."

Hermes turned to Athena. "And you?"

"I can give you great wisdom and battle skills," she said to the shepherd.

Without hesitation, Paris awarded the golden apple to Aphrodite.

Two years later, after Helen had been taken—or wooed—by Paris of Troy, the Greeks finally finished assembling their armies to retrieve her, for she had been married to Menelaus, brother to their king, Agamemnon. Athena, having joined forces with Hera to help the Greeks recover the stolen bride, was determined to enlist Odysseus from Ithaca. But Odysseus wished to avoid the war by pretending to be insane because of a prophecy predicting a long journey home for him if he went.

Athena searched for him for months—for both Odysseus and Prometheus. She finally spotted the former with a donkey pulling a lopsided plow sowing common table salt, to appear mad. She went to Hermes for help, and he came up with a scheme to inspire a prince to lay Odysseus's infant son in front of the plow. As Hermes had anticipated, Odysseus avoided his son, proving to everyone that he wasn't mad, and he was forced to join the effort.

For more than ten years, Athena poured herself into helping Odysseus and the other Greeks fight against the Trojans. All the while, she scanned the landscape for signs of Prometheus. Day after day, year after year, men died in the battlefield. She'd been certain that the Titan would come to the aid of his beloved creations, but the years wore on with no sign of him.

Rumors of a prophecy that Troy would not fall without the help of Achilles spurred Athena to help Odysseus find the young hero. He was the son of Thetis and Peleus, whose wedding party she'd been attending when Eris had dropped the dreaded golden apple that started this conflict in the first place. When months went by without any sign of Achilles, Athena once again went to Hermes for help.

But it was Odysseus who figured out how to find the young warrior. He'd heard that Thetis knew that if Achilles fought in the war, he would not survive. To protect her son, she'd convinced him to dress as a girl and live among the princesses on the island of Skyros. Odysseus hatched a plan to sail to Skyros disguised as a peddler of women's clothes and jewelry. Athena and Hermes followed, curious to watch the events unfold. They flew together across the Aegean Sea above the ship on which Odysseus had secured passage.

As she studied the men on deck, Athena had a shock. Standing with his crew, the captain possessed an uncanny resemblance to Prometheus. Was it possible they were one and the same?

Athena studied the captain from afar for many hours as they sailed toward Skyros, and the longer she observed him, the more certain she became that he was Prometheus. Helios gave a polite nod to her as he passed in his cup, and she wondered if he knew that the Titan whom his descent had once doomed was below him. Her heart raced, she was trembling slightly, and her ears were ringing as she debated what to do. Not knowing if she could trust Hermes to keep a secret from Zeus, she didn't share her suspicions with him. She also didn't want Prometheus to know that she'd found him—if, indeed, she had—because she feared he would avoid her by vanishing again.

She waited until the ship was anchored near the island and Odysseus and most of the crew had boarded the small boat that would go ashore. Fearing Hermes would recognize Prometheus with fewer men on board, she turned to him and said, "Will you stay with Odysseus while I remain with the ship? I have a bad feeling."

Hermes did as she asked. She waited until the boat reached the island and the men had climbed ashore before she allowed herself to sneak aboard the ship.

Suddenly fearing that Prometheus would sense her and flee, and she'd never get this close to finding him again, Athena sought Hermes at Skyros, where Odysseus was already among the princesses, trying to trick Achilles into revealing himself.

"Has something happened?" Hermes asked her where he stood hidden in the back of the room.

"I suspect one of the crew is planning a mutinous plot," she lied. "I want to put him into a deep slumber and interrogate him in his dream."

"Lead me to him," Hermes, who was responsible for bringing sleep and dreams to mortals, replied.

"You stay here in case Odysseus needs help," she insisted. "Isn't there something you can give me that will enable me to pull it off without you?"

"Why don't you stay with Odysseus, and I'll go question the crew member?"

"You don't know which one I suspect, and, besides, I want to do it. Can you help me?"

Hermes arched a brow and studied her with suspicion. After a few seconds, he sighed, conjured his staff, and handed it over to her. It was known as the caduceus and was made of two serpents intertwined and topped with wings. "Find the person you suspect and wave my staff over him. Once he's out, wave it again to conjure a dream. You can enter the dream, but if you don't want the sailor to remember it, you'll need to leave it before he awakes."

"How long will this staff keep him asleep?"

"There's no knowing for sure, Athena. His surroundings could wake him at any time. But the closer you get the staff to him, the more likely he'll remain asleep."

She wanted to ask if the effect was different on gods than on men, but not wanting to arouse his suspicion further, she thanked Hermes and left for the ship.

She scanned the deck for signs of the captain from a safe distance in the sky. Not finding him, she stole on board and cautiously crept toward the captain's quarters. As she pressed her ear to the wooden door, something brushed against her back, and the next thing she knew, she was lying on a bed in an unfamiliar room.

And Prometheus, holding the caduceus against her chest, stood over her.

"Hello, Athena."

Even though she'd suspected the captain to be him, she couldn't believe her eyes. "Prometheus? Is it really you?"

"You know it is. For once, I was unable to elude your tenacious searching. Why won't you please give up?"

She swallowed hard, trying to stop her lips from trembling. "I need to know if you still love me."

"It's better you don't know. If I say yes, you'll long for what you cannot have. If I say no, you'll grow bitter and resentful."

She tried to sit up but couldn't. That's when she knew she was dreaming. He was doing the very thing to her that she'd intended to do to him.

"If you say no, I'll move on," she promised.

Prometheus ran his fingers though his hair, wearing heartache on his face for the first time.

"But you can't, can you?" she said as love bloomed in her heart. "You're incapable of telling me a lie. Which means—"

Prometheus interrupted her speech by kissing her. His lips pressed softly at first, then harder and more passionately. With the staff of Hermes between them, he caressed her hair and spoke against her lips. "I long for you every single day. I try to distract myself from thoughts of you, but when I fail, I fail miserably."

She circled her arms around his neck, hardly able to believe what was happening.

"You stayed by my side for twenty years, enduring my torment with me," he said before kissing each of her cheeks. "Then you rescued me with the help of Heracles." He kissed her nose and her chin.

Tears of joy and sorrow spilled from the corners of her eyes. "Why have you put us through this further agony of being separated? We could be together, making one another happy."

"I do not trust your father. The torment he put me through was unbearable. It haunts me still."

She kissed his furrowed brow. "I'm so sorry that I couldn't bear the burden for you."

"I couldn't risk him tormenting me further, and you right alongside me by associating with me, his number-one enemy. That's what he called me, did you know? His number-one enemy."

She pulled his head closer, so she could kiss him again. "Let me decide my own fate, will you? Let me choose which risks are worth taking."

He kissed her hair, her forehead, her neck, and then returned his mouth to hers. She held his curly hair in her fists, wanting to hold him there against her forever.

"I swore an oath," he reminded her. "I must help you in any way I can."

She stopped kissing him to study his face. "You don't help me by vanishing."

"It's better than the alternative."

"Prometheus—"

"You won't remember any of this when you wake," he said. "So shut up and kiss me for the few moments we have left."

His mouth pressed firmly against hers, sending waves of heat throughout her body. She'd forgotten how much a kiss from him could affect every ounce of her flesh, every nerve, every muscle, every sinew. He lifted her head and pressed against her lips even harder, moving his tongue inside her mouth to sweep across her own.

"Oh, Prometheus," she whispered against his lips, her fingers digging into his biceps.

She moved her hands along his arms to his shoulders and then down his back, feeling every inch of him like a blind person using touch to understand the look of a person. Her fingers were both exploring and remembering.

As her hands moved down his back, a groan escaped from his throat, and he pressed his body hard against her, nearly driving the caduceus into her chest.

"Sweet Athena," he whispered.

"Athena, darling, wake up," a faraway voice insisted. "Athena?"

Athena opened her eyes to Hermes leaning over her.

"Where are we? What's happened?" she asked, finding herself in unfamiliar surroundings.

"I found you here in the captain's bed with my staff across your chest," the messenger god explained.

"I don't understand." The last thing she recalled was borrowing the staff with plans of using it on Prometheus.

Hermes cocked his head to the side. "You weren't completely honest with me, were you?"

She sat up and studied him. "Where's Odysseus?"

"On board. We're sailing toward Sparta."

"And Achilles?"

"Also on board."

She took a deep breath. "What about the captain?"

"Aye, the captain," Hermes said with a solemn nod. "He abandoned ship and left his first mate in charge. Any idea why?"

The blood left Athena's cheeks. "I think you know. I'm sorry I didn't tell you. I was afraid you'd tell Zeus."

"Prometheus got the better of you, it seems. He put you into the deep boon of sleep and made his escape."

"It seems so," she admitted.

"You're still in love with him, then?" Hermes asked tenderly.

The goddess frowned and said nothing for many seconds. When she finally met his gaze, she said, "I wish I could say no."

Hermes sighed. "So do I, darling Athena. So do I."

PART TWO: MODERN TIMES

CHAPTER THIRTEEN

Zeus's Number-One Enemy

Athena flew across the evening sky with Ares toward Mount Olympus after helping soldiers on both sides of the battlefield in the desert.

"Tough week," Ares said.

"It's never easy to watch mortals die."

"You did good out there."

She gave him a sideways glance. "Do you want something from me?"

Ares laughed, his vibrant, red hair blowing into his bright, blue eyes. "You are terrible at receiving compliments."

She grinned. "Especially those coming from you."

"Still no word from your mother?" Ares asked.

Athena's smile vanished. Seventeen years ago, Zeus had ruled that no more gods could be created, and he had commanded Hera, the goddess of marriage and family, to render all deities infertile. He feared the production of more gods would threaten his reign, and the Olympians, who preferred the stability of Zeus to a future unknown, had acquiesced. This had given Athena an opportunity she had never believed possible. She could argue for her mother's freedom.

But things had not gone as planned.

"No," she lied to Ares, for she had secretly visited her mother a week ago and had another appointment with her that very night. She glanced at Ares, wondering if he could see through her lie. "No, I have not."

In the dark of night, Athena flew to her mother's secret hiding spot, a cave on a remote island in the Arabian Sea. She was grateful for the clouds that shielded her from the view of Selene, flying far above them in her chariot. When Athena reached the mouth of the cave, her mother, hooded and somber, was waiting.

"Come in," Metis said.

Athena hated the distance between them. While she had been trapped inside her father, she had never imagined there would come a time when she wouldn't long to embrace her mother, when she wouldn't shower her face with kisses.

They navigated through a series of long, winding tunnels. Some parts required them to stoop, and still others were filled with at least five inches of water.

"You're certain no one followed?" her mother asked.

"I'm certain."

They finally came to the chamber where her mother lived. Athena took a seat on a couch across from the fire crackling in the hearth. "You promised to tell me the truth."

Metis removed her hood and cloak, laid it across the back of the couch, and sat in a chair, where she stoked the fire. Her raven hair fell across her shoulders. She was still beautiful, even after so many years.

No, Athena thought, it wasn't her mother's beauty that had faded.

"Is it true, what they're saying?" Athena asked. "Did you really use dark magic to conceive a son with Zeus?"

Metis met her eyes. "You already know the answer to that question. Why else would I be in hiding away from you for fifteen long years?"

"*Sixteen* long years," Athena corrected.

Her mother frowned. "I'm always thinking of you. Never doubt it."

It was too late for that. "I have a brother, then?"

"Indeed."

"Where is he?"

"You know better than to ask me that."

Athena felt her throat get tight and her breath quicken as she clenched her fists and jaw. "Why would you do this, Mother? I don't understand."

Metis glared at her. "How can you defend your father after what he's put you through—put *us* through?"

"He does what he must to secure his reign."

"And Prometheus's punishment? Was that necessary? Especially when Zeus knew what the Titan meant to you?"

Athena bowed her head and said nothing.

Metis added, "I see your armor has served you well."

"Yes."

"Your father doesn't deserve your love."

Athena looked up at her mother and gasped. "And you do? After what you've done? All that talk in my father's belly, and later from behind his eyes, about longing to be near me, and not a year after your release, you disappear without a word. You've betrayed everyone, Mother. You've betrayed us all."

"I'm saving you," she insisted. "I'm saving every last one of you from a tyrannical ruler."

Athena jumped to her feet. "How can you believe such a thing when you know that no one stands with you? This can only end badly, Mother. I thought you were wiser than this."

"Why do you assume I have no allies?" Metis challenged. "Do you really think so little of me?"

Athena covered her mouth and returned to the couch. "Who?"

"If I knew I could trust you, I'd divulge everything, my dear. I have no guarantee that you won't go straight to your father and ruin everything."

Tears of frustration formed in Athena's eyes. "You were the one who told me to stay close to him."

"So that you would be close to *me,*" her mother growled, startling her.

Athena sat quietly, staring at the fire, wondering who her mother's allies were. There was no way Ares or Hermes would ever betray their father. She considered each of the Olympians and hadn't gotten very far when her mother came and sat beside her.

"Oh, Athena, just imagine a world in which things are different. Your brother is unlike your father in every way. He doesn't even want to rule. But if he fulfills his destiny and deposes Zeus, imagine what that would mean for you."

"The loss of one of my parents?" she chided.

"The gain of your heart's true love."

Athena sucked in air, nearly choking on it.

"Think of it, my dear. There would be nothing preventing you and Prometheus from being together."

"Why do you think either of us wants that after all these years?"

Her mother pushed a strand of Athena's hair behind her ear, a tenderness Athena hadn't felt from her in ages. "I still know you, daughter."

"It makes no difference if I'm the only one who wants it."

Her mother gave her a curious smile.

Athena's brows lifted as suspicions she could never have fathomed before washed over her. "Mother? Do you know where Prometheus is? Have you been in contact with him?"

"Indeed, I have, my darling girl. He has been training your brother these past five years."

Athena sat in stunned silence for many seconds. Then, grabbing her mother's shoulders, she urged, "Where is he? If you ever loved me, tell me where he is."

"Of course, I love you. I love your brother, too, and need to know I can trust you. I won't endanger him."

"They're together *now*? He and Prometheus?"

"They are."

Athena bit her lip. "You've heard about the prophecy, haven't you? About the twins of Thanatos?"

Metis nodded. "Apollo isn't the only one who sees it. Prometheus has seen it, too."

"That's how Zeus will find him," Athena said as a knot formed in her stomach. She released her mother's shoulders and paced before the hearth. "He knows that if he keeps his eye on the twins of Thanatos, they'll eventually lead him to Prometheus."

Thanatos and Hypnos were the twin sons of Hades and Persephone, and after they were born, they took over the duties of death and sleep from Hermes. The children of Thanatos had been seen in a vision by Apollo, which had given Zeus the hope of finally capturing his number-one enemy once and for all.

If Prometheus had returned to Mount Olympus that somber day when Heracles had freed him, he would have been welcomed back into the fold—according to her father. The Titan's decision to flee is what had convinced Zeus that Prometheus was conspiring to seek his revenge.

Apparently, her father had been right.

"Oh, Mother. What can we do?"

"I need you to do something to prove your loyalty to me," Metis explained. "Then, and only then, will I tell you the plan."

Should she really do this—betray her father for her mother and Prometheus? Betray the rest of the Olympians? Was she prepared to become a traitor? Did she have it in her?

"What would you have me do?" Athena asked, still not committed to the idea, but wanting the information so she could make a better decision.

"I need you to lure Hermes into a trap."

Her eyes widened. "Hermes? Why?"

"If we can't recruit him to our side—"

"You can't recruit Hermes."

"Then I'll claim that you're my prisoner, too, and trade the two of you for Apollo."

"Zeus won't make that trade, Mother. Why would he? Apollo's visions are too valuable."

"So are speed and wisdom. Besides, you and Hermes are his favorites."

"He won't make that trade."

"Nevertheless, that's what I need you to do, if you want to know where Poros and Prometheus are hiding."

"Poros? That's my brother's name?"

Her mother nodded with a smile. "He's a remarkable young man. I'd love for you to know him."

Athena sighed. She'd love to know him, too. "What trap do you have planned for Hermes?"

"You must swear your loyalty to me on the River Styx, and then I'll tell you. Once you prove your oath by entrapping him, I'll know you're on my side, and I'll divulge the rest of the plan."

"Let me give this some thought."

"Return tomorrow night with your answer."

Except for her father and Hera, the great hall of Mount Olympus was quiet when Athena returned. The other gods were either in their rooms or down below carrying out their duties among mortals.

"Hello, Athena," her father said cheerfully from where he sat beside Hera on his throne. "Ares said there was quite a bit of turmoil this week in the desert."

"It won't be ending anytime soon, unfortunately," Athena said.

"You have a favorite?" he asked.

"Not this time," she admitted. "I see honor on both sides but no hope of a peaceful resolution."

Her comment had been about the war in the desert, but it could also be applied to her own situation.

"Where are you coming from?" Hera asked. "Ares arrived home hours ago."

She did not like Hera's suspicious tone, nor did she feel obligated to answer; however, not wanting to arouse further suspicion, she shrugged and said, "I was scouting for heroes, as I often do."

"You were looking for Prometheus," Hera accused.

"We should all be looking for him," Zeus declared. "The children of Thanatos have reached the age that they appear in Apollo's vision. We must all be on guard against Prometheus, right Athena? He's the number-one threat to this regime."

"Of course," she said, meeting his gaze.

Even after all these years, she still found herself searching for her mother behind his eyes.

"I am proud of the warrior goddess you've become," her father said. "Ares sang your praises tonight."

"Thank you," she said, hiding the surprise from her voice.

"I can still recall the first time I laid eyes on you," he added, "covered in my blood and wearing your armor. You came into this world ready to fight, didn't you, my dear?"

"I do what I must," she conceded. "It seems a necessary evil."

Her father gave her a solemn nod. "Indeed. Well put."

"Good night," she said to them. "I'm off to bed."

"Sweet dreams, my dear," Zeus said affectionately, causing Athena's stomach to knot.

How could she betray her father?

Tired after a long week on the battlefield and overwhelmed after her visit to her mother's cave, Athena flew to her rooms, removed her boots and armor, and lay on her bed.

She did not pray to Hypnos, the god of sleep, immediately, for she needed time to process her conversation with her mother and the news her mother had revealed. Metis knew the whereabouts of Prometheus. That alone was mind-boggling and gut-wrenching. Athena had searched for centuries to no avail, and now her very own mother knew his location. Athena could see him again, could touch him again, and perhaps, if he allowed it, could love him again. But at what price?

She covered her face, wishing her mother loved her enough to reveal the Titan's location without a condition—a condition which would require her to completely upturn her world by betraying the one parent who had been there for her. When Athena had convinced Zeus to free Metis, her mother had been reluctant to leave his belly. Then, once the goddess had been coaxed out, she'd remained at Mount Olympus for less than a year before vanishing without any explanation to Athena or anyone. Athena had spent the next year searching for *two* lost loves. And there'd been no sign, no trail, not a clue until Uranus, disguised as Aether, had kidnapped Hypnos and, along with Metis, had attempted a coup that had come alarmingly close to succeeding. Defeated, Uranus was captured, and Metis vanished again.

While in captivity, Hypnos had learned of Metis's pregnancy by Zeus using dark magic. Prometheus had been demoted to Zeus's number-two enemy, and every deity for the last fifteen years had been on the hunt for Metis.

Apollo's vision of Prometheus with the twins of Thanatos had changed the primary focus back to the Titan. And now Athena knew that the two were connected. Metis and Prometheus were in cahoots to overthrow her father.

In fact, according to her mother, Prometheus had been training Athena's now fifteen-year-old brother, Poros. And there were other mysterious allies Metis had already recruited.

Moreover, if Athena wished to learn the whereabouts of Prometheus and her brother from her mother, she must swear her allegiance on the River Styx. Then, she must prove that loyalty by luring Hermes into a trap.

The thought of betraying her father and the other Olympians, who she knew would never support her mother and brother, made her feel sick.

But of all the thoughts swirling through her mind, one among them dominated the others and soon became her singular focus: her mother believed Athena and Prometheus might one day be reunited. Dare she allow herself to imagine the possibility?

She prayed to Hypnos to bring her sleep and to put her out of her misery, and she also prayed for dreams from bygone days when she and Prometheus were together. What harm was there in dreaming?

Athena was eating her breakfast in the garden behind the great temple when Hermes approached.

"Good morning, Athena."

"Good morning. You're in a good mood."

"I should be." He sat in the golden chair across from her, and the honeysuckle vines that grew around the trellis of the gazebo tickled his shoulder. "I just returned from a fishing trip with Hecate."

"Is it springtime already?"

Hecate's presence on Mount Olympus coincided with Persephone's. They were only ever there six months out of the year. The rest of the time was spent with Hades in the Underworld.

"It is. And March is the best month for freshwater fishing."

"You must have caught quite a few to be wearing such a big grin."

"We caught a few, but that's not what has me grinning."

"Oh?"

Hermes laughed. "You should have seen her."

"Hecate?"

He nodded. "I told her about this woman I know."

Athena smirked. "I hear you know a lot of them."

Hermes laughed again. "Guilty as charged. Guilty as charged. But this woman preferred a python to any man."

Athena narrowed her eyes. "I hope you're not saying—"

"What? Oh, gods, no. But she did love this python. For weeks she fed it live rabbits, rats, and mice. She fed it like a baby. And every night, she slept with it in her bed, stroking it—more like a child than a lover. Get your head out of the gutter."

"It's not my head we should worry about."

"Touché. Anyway, one day the snake refused its meal. And this went on for days and then for weeks. Eventually, the woman took her python to the vet to see if the doctor could explain why."

"And?"

"The vet examined the snake from top to bottom and said to the woman, 'This python is perfectly healthy but has completely emptied its stomach. Pythons only ever do this when they're preparing for a very large meal.'"

Athena sat upright. "No!"

"The vet added, 'I would not advise you to continue to sleep with it.'"

Athena shuddered. "How terrifying for the woman."

"I haven't even gotten to the good part, Athena."

"I'm listening."

"While I was telling this story to Hecate, we were sitting on the bank of a river fishing, and Dionysus, who was in on it, was hiding beneath the helm."

"Hades let you borrow the helm?"

"No one gives that god enough credit. He can be fun when given the chance."

"I highly doubt that."

"Anyway, beneath the helm, Dionysus was holding this huge python, and just when I got to the part about the vet advising the woman—"

Athena covered her mouth. "No way."

Hermes busted out laughing again. "You should have seen her. She jumped so high in the sky, that she nearly upset Helios in his chariot!"

Athena couldn't help but laugh right alongside Hermes as she imagined the goddess of the crossroads and witchcraft reacting to the python. As she laughed with her friend, her brother, and her sometime charmer, she realized that there was no way she could bring herself to betray him, no matter how badly her heart desired Prometheus. She must refuse her mother's offer.

This thought quickly sobered her.

"Everything okay?" Hermes asked, noticing a change in her expression.

She sighed, not sure how to reply.

"You're worried about Prometheus," he deduced. "Of course, you are. I'm sure this is a difficult time for you."

Athena was moved by his compassion.

"I wish there was something I could do," he added. "I can only imagine how miserable you must feel, knowing that he's Zeus's number-one enemy again."

"It wasn't any easier when that position was held by my mother," she pointed out. "But nothing rarely is easy, is it?"

"That trick I played today was," he said with a gleam in his eyes. "Oh, if you'd have seen it, you'd still be laughing."

"I wish I had."

That night, Athena, sadder than she'd felt in decades, flew to the Arabian Sea to give her mother her answer. She would not swear her loyalty. She would not trap Hermes. She would remain true to her father and to the other Olympians. But her heart was heavy, and though her eyes were dry, she felt on the verge of tears as she waited at the entrance to her mother's cave.

Her mother, hooded, appeared as she had the previous night. "Come inside."

Athena followed her through the winding tunnels toward her mother's dwelling and was soon shocked by what she saw. Standing beside the hearth with its glowing, crackling fire was Prometheus.

CHAPTER FOURTEEN

A Bittersweet Reunion

I'll leave you two to catch up," Metis said before she disappeared down another winding tunnel in the back of her cave.

"Hi, Athena," Prometheus said once they were alone. "It's good to see you."

Athena glared at him. "It might have been sooner."

"Don't be angry with me." He took a step closer to her, and she backed away. "You must understand that everything I did was for you."

A harsh laugh gurgled from Athena's throat. "Since when did you become a smooth talker? It just proves that you're not the same person I fell in love with. Thank you for making it easier for me to walk away."

She turned to leave.

"Wait. Please, hear me out."

He took her hand—which was trembling, something that made her even angrier. Why couldn't she control her own hand?

"You searched for me for centuries, and now that we're together, you're going to leave without hearing what I have to say?" He led her to sit beside him on the couch, and she dumbly followed.

"What makes you think I searched for you for centuries? How do you know I didn't give up a very long time ago?"

He smiled gently, as if he were talking to a child. "I've seen you. I've spent my time looking out for you, hoping to catch a glimpse of you before having to disappear again."

"I don't believe you."

"It's true. I never stopped loving you."

She refused to believe it. "You just want my help in deposing my father."

It was his turn to glare. "I can't believe you would think that of me."

"I hardly know you anymore."

"That's not true, Athena. I'm the same. The very same."

He looked the same—or nearly so. He wore his dark, curly hair and beard long, but his dark eyes that peered down at her from beneath even darker brows were the same. His mouth, his jaw, the cut of his build—these were the same.

Perhaps he noticed her admiring him, for his face softened, and he squeezed her hand. "My sweet Athena. I can hardly believe we're alone together."

She jumped from the couch and moved to the hearth, staring at the dancing flames. Conflicting emotions coursed through her, and she felt dizzy and on the verge of fainting.

"Are you really not happy to see me?" he asked. "Do you have no love for me, Athena?"

"You took a rare, incredible, profound thing and you twisted it," she accused as she fought tears, all the while keeping her back to him. "By depriving us of one another's company, conversation, touch . . . You ruined something beautiful."

"Don't say that. It was deferred, not ruined."

"Ruined," she insisted. "Think of all the years we might have shared together. Think how different our lives might have been."

She suddenly had the strangest sense of déjà vu, as if she'd said those very words to him before.

"Immortality is a long time," he insisted. "I wanted you free and safe, which you could not be at my side while your father reigned."

"What about what I wanted?"

"I never believed we wouldn't one day reunite."

She chewed on the inside of her lower lip and held onto the mantle over the hearth for support. "You never thought to share that with me?"

"I wanted you to have the chance to live more than the shadow life that I have lived."

She turned to face him. "Impossible. That was impossible. And you made it impossible."

"You became a great warrior and a powerful leader," he argued. "You are the most beloved of the Olympians."

"A shadow life. That's what you cursed me with. You cursed us both."

"It could have been worse. We might have been swallowed, thrown into the Titan Pit, ripped to shreds by the Maenads."

"We'll never know what might have been. You gave us no such chance."

He took a step toward her. She backed against the hearth, nearly burning her flesh in the flames.

"Athena, please," he said softly. "Please forgive me. I did what I thought was best for you. Not just for you, but for all of us and all people. I was preparing for the coming of your brother and for the change that would liberate us all, a time when we could finally be together without fear, without looking over our shoulders."

He'd been planning this from the start? Athena studied him, as if she were looking at him for the first time.

"Your father is a selfish ruler, Athena. You are wise enough to know that the best rulers love their people more than they love themselves."

"What's my brother like?"

He smiled warmly, obviously fond of the boy. "His hair is the color of sand. But he has your gray eyes and your strength. He has wisdom, too, without ambition. He has utterly no desire to rule anyone or anything. It's amazing that he came from your father."

"If he has no desire to rule, why would he agree to overthrow Zeus?"

"He wants to do it for you."

Athena gasped. "For me? What do you mean?"

"He knows your story. He wants to give your father a chance to make amends, and when he doesn't—like we know he won't—Poros will fulfill his destiny and install you as the new leader of the Olympians."

Athena's eyes widened with shock and alarm. "Me? What? I will not betray my father. I came here to say that very thing to my mother."

She was surprised when Prometheus grinned. "But you do, Athena. You will. I've seen it."

"Only the Fates know for certain what the future holds," she snapped.

"True."

"Besides, I would have thought you'd want the throne for yourself."

Prometheus laughed. "I'm like your brother. I have no desire to rule. I just want a better, more just leader. That could be you, Athena."

"I will not depose my father."

"Please think about it before you give Metis your answer. Take some more time, I beg of you. Imagine how things might be if we were out from beneath your father's tyranny."

She'd been about to object to his use of the word *tyranny* but then recalled the many years she stood beside him as her father's eagle came at sunset to peck out his liver.

"Don't get your hopes up," she warned. "Tell my mother that I'll return in a week with my answer."

"Thank you," he said. "That means a lot to me—that you will at least think about it."

"Like I said, don't get your hopes up. I'm not the same person you fell in love with."

With that, Athena rushed from the cave, through its winding tunnels, and into the night, but even in that fresh air, filled with the arrival of spring, Athena could not breathe.

CHAPTER FIFTEEN

Wolves and Innuendo

Athena was surprised the next day when Artemis appeared outside her chamber door and called to her.

"Athena," she spoke with urgency, "we must act swiftly. A pack of wolves has been terrorizing a small farming community nearby. They've grown bold, attacking livestock, and are now endangering the lives of the people."

The goddess of wisdom quickly dressed in her armor and boots, grabbed her spear, and opened the door to her sister. "Lead the way."

With Artemis guiding the path, they ventured through the verdant forests and winding trails to a small village deep in the heart of Greece, where the low, guttural growls of nearly a dozen wolves echoed across the landscape.

Above the sound of the wolves could be heard the sharp cries of a small child from inside an old chicken coop, its frame splintered and broken. The child was visible and vulnerable, the coop offering him no protection from the wolves that were circling it.

Half a dozen chickens lay dead and half-eaten on the ground. Two men stood nearby on the back of a pickup truck, their rifles aimed and ready. Athena could hear their prayers, which were riddled with the fear that if they were to shoot, they would frighten the toddler, who might run from the coop and be instantly snatched by the vicious beasts—or worse, run into the line of fire and be killed by their own bullets.

Inside the truck behind the steering wheel sat a woman sobbing her eyes out and trembling like a bare branch in the winter winds. She was the mother, and her desperate prayers were addressed to any god who would listen.

Without hesitation, Athena and Artemis sprang into action. Athena gripped her spear, its gleaming tip catching the sunlight as she surveyed their surroundings with steely resolve. Artemis notched an arrow to her bow, her keen eyes scanning the ground for any sign of movement.

The wolves sensed the goddesses, for their fur bristled, and their growls grew louder and more intense.

With a silent nod from Artemis, Athena advanced. She and her sister positioned themselves between the child and the wolves.

As the first wolf lunged forward, Athena met its charge with a swift thrust of her spear, its razor-sharp point finding its mark with deadly precision. As she thrust it into the breast of the beast, she threw her anger and frustration with Prometheus into the act. It was satisfying to vent her emotions this way, and she smiled as the beast howled in agony and fell, its lifeblood staining the earth beneath its feet.

Artemis, ever the agile huntress, let loose a volley of arrows that sailed through the air like streaks of lightning, each one finding its target with unerring accuracy. With each shot, she struck down another of the savage predators.

Athena drove her spear again and again, fighting not just against the wolves, but against the chains of fate that bound her to a destiny she had not chosen. Again, she asked herself why Prometheus had made his decision without consulting her, as if he alone had known what was best for her. In that moment, she felt a kinship with the warriors she had been helping alongside Ares in the desert, understanding the relief they must have felt with each blow.

But even as they fought, the wolves closed in, their snarls growing ever closer as they circled their prey with deadly intent. Athena growled back at the beasts as she lunged with her spear, again and again, as Artemis shot off her arrows.

In the next instant, it was over. The beasts lay in pools of blood with the half-eaten chickens. The child's cries continued to pierce the air. Athena flew to the boy and lifted him from the dilapidated coop and carried him safely to his mother's arms.

The mortals fell to their knees and thanked the goddesses.

Their breaths ragged and their bodies weary from the struggle, the sister goddesses left the farmers and flew toward Mount Olympus.

"That felt good," Athena said.

"Yes. I'm glad you were at home. I couldn't find Apollo and knew I'd risk the child's life if I attempted to fight the wolves alone."

"We made a great team."

Artemis flashed her a smile. "I've been meaning to say something to you, Athena."

"Oh?" Athena noticed a shadow of uncertainty on her sister's features.

Artemis seemed to choose her words carefully and with hesitance. "I understand the complexities of family ties. Your family, for example, is more complex than most."

"I don't get your meaning."

Artemis cleared her throat, glanced away, and then said softly, "The bonds that bind us to those we love can often lead us down paths we never imagined."

Athena's eyes widened with shock. Was Artemis trying to tell her that she was one of Metis's mysterious allies?

"What are you trying to say, Artemis?"

The goddess of the hunt moved closer to her as they flew across the heavens, their shoulders touching. "I overheard Hera talking to Aphrodite this morning. Zeus will soon be calling a meeting on

Mount Olympus to discuss your mother and brother and to question the loyalty of the members of the Olympian court."

The blood left Athena's face. She should have seen this coming.

"And I'm trying to say," the goddess continued, "that loyalty isn't as simple as it seems and that some might oppose our father, not out of malice or hatred, but out of a desire for a greater sense of justice and freedom."

Telepathically, Athena asked her sister, *Are you with my mother and Prometheus?*

Artemis lifted her brows. "I don't know what you mean." Then, telepathically, she asked, *Are you?*

I do not know, Athena replied.

Then we shall speak no more about it until you do, Artemis insisted.

Alone in the sanctity of her chambers atop Mount Olympus, Athena immersed herself in the soothing waters of her marble bath, the fragrant scent of wildflowers mingling with the steam that rose around her. Yet amidst the tranquil embrace of the fragrant steam, her thoughts remained consumed by the weight of her conversations with her mother, Prometheus, and Artemis.

Betrayal, loyalty, duty . . . The words echoed in the recesses of her mind, each one a poignant reminder of the choice that lay before her. Shouldn't she stand by her father and the Olympian pantheon, unwavering in her allegiance to the throne of Zeus? But could she turn her back on her mother, the brother she'd never met, and the lover who stole her heart centuries ago?

She supposed that her answer might be easier if she knew who her mother's allies were. Perhaps taking her mother's side was not the same as betraying the Olympians, if enough of them were done with Zeus. Who besides Artemis had already turned against him—if indeed the huntress had?

Athena closed her eyes and lay back, her head resting on the marble ledge. Allowing the water, the fragrance, and the silence to envelop her, Athena sought to clear her mind and give herself a reprieve from the thoughts swirling there. She focused on her breathing and on the rise and fall of her chest.

Her quiet solitude was shattered by a horn sounding throughout the temple. It was only used for urgent meetings with the council. Artemis had been right. Zeus was gathering the Olympians, which meant that she had no more time to ponder.

Athena put on fresh clothes and then her armor and boots and headed to the council meeting. To her surprise, most of the others were already there talking among themselves. She took her seat on her father's right, meeting his affectionate smile with her own. Her stomach formed a knot. She loved her father despite his shortcomings. He had managed to maintain centuries of peace among the gods.

Artemis shot her a knowing glance. Athena gave her a smile but said nothing.

After several more minutes of idle chatter had passed, Zeus stood on the dais before his throne and lifted his arms in the air.

"Thank you for gathering here with me today," he said. "We have a sensitive matter to discuss."

The great hall became quiet, and all eyes turned to their leader.

"As you have heard by now, our great pantheon is in jeopardy," Zeus continued. "Metis disguised herself as my beloved Hera and deceived me into lying with her. She used dark magic to become pregnant, and it's been confirmed that she bore a son, who is now of age."

A cacophony of whispers erupted, but Zeus raised his arms again and quieted the room.

"A prophecy was first told by Prometheus while I was married to Metis and again later while he was still chained to the mountain and serving his punishment for treason. The son of Metis would overthrow me."

More whispers erupted, so Zeus lifted his arms.

"As you know, only the Fates know with certainty what the future brings," he said. "Our way of life is not doomed. We can fight."

Now applause broke out, and the expressions of many transformed into hopeful smiles.

"Hear, hear!" Aphrodite shouted.

"Defend Olympus!" Ares yelled.

"Hooray!" others cried out.

Athena noted which among the Olympians did not cheer—Artemis and her brother were silent, as were Poseidon and Hades. Could this mean they had already been recruited by Metis?

Zeus basked in the cheers for a while before lifting his hands again for silence.

"I have no doubt that we can defend our way of life, but only if we are vigilant and prepared," Zeus said. "Right now, I have spies working night and day, collecting information for our cause. For example, I'm sorry to report that we now know Gaia is against us."

Shouts of reproach resounded throughout the hall.

"How could she?" Aphrodite cried.

"Our own Mother Earth, a traitor?" Hermes asked, incredulously.

Athena covered her mouth and gasped. Was Gaia with her mother and Prometheus? What spy had uncovered this—if it were even true?

Zeus raised his hands and continued, "We have also discovered that Hecate sent a secret code to the children of Thanatos claiming that Prometheus is not their enemy."

Athena straightened her back. Why would Hecate do such a thing unless she was an ally of Metis?

"She is now serving a sentence in the Titan pit," Zeus added.

Athena looked across the great hall at Hermes whose face was as white as sea foam. Then she turned to Demeter. The goddess of the harvest and her daughter huddled together on their double throne weeping inconsolably.

"Unfortunately," Zeus continued, "the intelligence collected by my spies has cast a shadow of suspicion over this court as well. Signs indicate that there may be traitors among us, in this very room."

From the crowd came sounds of disbelief and confusion, of smacks, of hisses, and of groans. Gods and goddesses gazed suspiciously at their neighbors. Athena exchanged a worried glance with Artemis.

Zeus raised his hands to silence the room.

"So that we might put to rest those fears and doubts, I have asked you to come and swear your allegiance to me and to this court on the River Styx."

Rhea, the mother of Zeus and his siblings, lifted her hands. "Please do not make the same mistake as your father."

"Which one, Mother?" Zeus asked warily. "He made more than even a god can count."

"The mistake of putting his crown before his family," she said.

Zeus's mouth dropped open. "Do you expect me to hand over my throne to my son?"

"If it better serves your family to do so, yes," she said.

"If it better serves my family?" he repeated angrily. "How could that possibly better serve my family?" His voice betrayed his rage. "I saved my family from your husband! I overthrew that wicked Titan. And I have ruled in all ways opposite to him, have I not? I have created a more democratic system in what was once a traditional monarchy! This council is proof of that. What king gives up some of his power if not a good one?"

Before Rhea could say more, Zeus continued, "I will not roll over and play dead like an old dog so that my inexperienced son can steal the leadership of this council from me." He grabbed a lightning bolt from behind his throne. He shouted, "I refuse!" and thrust it into the sky over Mount Olympus.

The bolt exploded into a thunderous burst of light, shaking the palace walls.

"I want to know who's loyal to me," Zeus said less angrily. "That is the sole purpose of this meeting. Is it too much to ask each of you to swear your allegiance on the River Styx? Would anyone here deny me that?"

"I don't think it's too much to ask, Lord Zeus," Morpheus, the god of dreams, declared.

"You, there, Morpheus," Zeus said. "You haven't disappointed me once since we brought you into the fold. The newest god among us is prepared to swear his allegiance! Let him be an example to the rest of you!"

A huge prideful grin spread across Morpheus's face. Iris kissed his cheek.

Poseidon stood before his throne. "Dear brother," he said to Zeus. "The problem with ordering everyone to swear their allegiance on the River Styx is this: They could lie. They could be willing to suffer the consequences of the Maenads as an oath breaker, like Thanatos once did, to hide their guilt. You'll be no more the wiser. So why command actions that will serve no worthwhile purpose?"

"Ah, Poseidon," Zeus said, narrowing his eyes at the god of the sea. "You bring up an interesting point. But, you see, this is where Apollo comes in. No one can lie before Apollo."

Everyone turned their eyes to Apollo, who sat looking as pale as a ghost.

The god of music, of light, and of truth stepped down from his throne and walked to the center of the court, where he faced his father. "I have something to say."

"Is it another vision?" Zeus asked eagerly.

"No," Apollo said. "It's a confession."

Apollo began to sing:

The last-born son of Kronos is the mightiest of all.
When he wields his thunderous lightning bolt,
And thrusts it into the heavens,
Any god or mortal in its wake is sure to fall.

Father to many and leader of all,
When he rules from his throne on Olympus,
His eagle soars the heavens,
And every god and mortal looks up to Zeus in awe.

His enemies fear him, as do those who follow him,
For he is the most powerful deity above;
Yet, he is my father, and, more than his might,
I want his love…

Familial love has escaped us for these many centuries.
Every god for himself or for herself,
Each one of us self-serving.
Today I will put an end to those miseries.

I choose love…
I choose love over power…
I choose love.

When Apollo had finished, Zeus looked down at him from where he stood on his throne and asked, "What are you saying, Apollo?"

Apollo glanced around at all present in the room, and it was then that Athena noticed the tears falling down the healing god's cheeks.

Apollo cleared his throat. "I can no longer serve you, Father."

Athena glanced at Artemis who met her eyes with a steely look.

"What? This is an outrage!" Hera cried.

"You can't be serious!" Ares shouted.

Hermes stepped from his throne toward Apollo. "Brother, think this through."

"I have," Apollo said, his face twisted in agony. "And I am serious. We need a pantheon that puts the needs of others first, that listens to the prayers of mortals and acts on them when possible."

Demeter stood on her throne. "How dare you? I answer prayers all the time."

"For half the year, you listen to no one," Apollo pointed out.

Demeter gaped. Then she cried, "Who are you to stand there and judge?"

"I am just as guilty," Apollo admitted. "I don't deny it. But I'm ready to change. I hope others among you are also ready. We needn't go to war."

"I will not step aside," Zeus said through gritted teeth.

"I will not serve you," Apollo repeated. "You are not the right leader for the change. You're too impulsive, selfish, disloyal—"

"Stop!" Hera demanded.

"Apollo, please!" Aphrodite cried.

Zeus's face turned white, and then, just as quickly, red as fresh blood. "You choose to turn your back on me, your own father? How can you do such a thing?"

"Like you did to Poros, your son?" Apollo asked, through tears.

"Poros?" Zeus repeated. To himself, he muttered, "So that's his name." Louder to Apollo, he asked, "You've seen him? What's he like?"

"Just and wise, like his sister," Apollo said.

Athena covered her mouth with a trembling hand.

Apollo continued, "He isn't self-serving—far from it. He doesn't want to rule."

"What does he want?" Zeus asked.

"To replace you with another," Apollo said.

"With whom?" Zeus demanded, still red-faced.

Athena clenched her fists and prayed to Apollo not to say her name.

"He wants the council to vote," Apollo said.

"Please don't do this!" Hestia cried.

"You could run for the position, Father," Apollo added. "We needn't go to war."

"I will not step aside," Zeus said again.

"I will not serve you without the vote." Then Apollo shouted to the others, "You wanted democracy! What Zeus has created is but a show of it. We all know his word remains absolute."

Zeus shouted, "Put him in the trick chair and silence him!"

"This is our chance!" Apollo shouted again. "For true democracy!"

Ares and his sons overtook Apollo, who did not resist. They gagged him and threw him into the trick chair near the center of the room. Hermes helped.

Athena felt paralyzed and speechless as she watched the events unfold before her.

"There's no point in swearing now," Poseidon pointed out.

"You're eager to avoid it, brother," Zeus accused.

Poseidon's face turned red as he bellowed, "I have duties to return to. This is a waste of time. I've grown weary of your paranoia, brother!"

Poseidon vanished. Murmurs took over the hall.

Zeus finally said, "We'll adjourn for now, but this council is on high alert."

As the others dispersed, Artemis prayed telepathically to Athena: *Please say yes and help my brother.*

CHAPTER SIXTEEN

Apollo

As Athena flew alongside Ares in the desert watching over, and sometimes interceding in, the war among mortals, her mind was elsewhere. The day before, she had asked Artemis to confide in her, to tell her who was conspiring against their father. Artemis had pretended that she didn't know what Athena was talking about.

"How should I know?" Artemis had asked defensively. "Am I my brother's keeper?"

Athena had gone to sleep feeling anxious and perturbed but had awakened that morning with an idea. She could borrow the caduceus from Hermes and put Apollo into the deep boon of sleep. Because it was impossible for Apollo to avoid the truth, she could ask him to tell her everything he knew.

But how could she convince Hermes to let her borrow his staff without raising his suspicion? If she admitted her motives, he might insist on being present. Even worse, he might alert Zeus. If so, Athena would expose her mother's allies in one fell swoop without knowing for certain whether she herself should be one of them.

She needed to think of a way to lead Hermes to believe that she was using the caduceus on someone else. But who? And why?

Then, it hit her. She would pretend to want to interrogate Poseidon. She would insist that she needed to know the truth about Medusa. Had the god of the seas abused the priestess?

Athena and Ares stayed with the troops on both sides of the war for a week before returning home to Mount Olympus. When she found that Hermes was not at home, she went looking for him.

She soon found him holding a massive 747 airplane jet up over his head and flying across South America.

"Hermes? What's happened?" she asked as she moved beside him to shoulder some of the weight.

"One of the engines blew and the plane was wobbling erratically. We just need to stabilize it long enough for them to land in Brazil."

Athena could now hear the desperate prayers of the passengers who feared for their lives.

"Down there," Hermes said, motioning his head toward an airport runway. "Time to land."

"You got it."

As they turned the nose of the plane down, the vessel rocked forward and back before stabilizing again, causing the passengers aboard to scream and groan. But soon after, Athena and Hermes had a good handle on the situation. They were able to ease the plane down onto the landing strip. The pilot smashed on the brakes and took it from there.

"Thanks," Hermes said to her.

"I know you could have easily done the job without me. Where are you headed next?"

"Home. But I have a feeling you came to me for a reason."

Athena grinned. "Perhaps for an opportunity to take in your good looks?"

Hermes threw his head back and guffawed. "Yeah, right. Sounds like it's a big favor you've come to ask for."

"It is." As they flew toward Mount Olympus, she told him the story of needing closure regarding Medusa.

Hermes clicked his tongue and shook his head. "Never lie to a liar. That was ages ago. You'd have wanted closure before now. Tell me why you really want my staff."

The color drained from Athena's face. "Okay, but you must swear to tell no one."

"I can't do that—not now when a rebellion is afoot."

Athena sighed. "Okay, fine. I want to question Apollo. I hope to learn who the other rebels are. But I don't want our father to know until I've had a chance to convince each traitor to return to the fold."

Athena felt guilty for lying again, but what choice did she have? Hermes would never betray their father.

Hermes seemed to consider her request. He didn't speak for quite some time as they continued alongside one another toward their home. Athena held her tongue, trying to give him the time he needed to decide for himself.

When they reached the gates of Mount Olympus, he said, "Okay, but I want to be there with you."

Athena's stomach lurched. It was too late to pull out now. If she didn't question Apollo, Hermes would do it without her.

"Okay," she agreed, wondering how in the world she would stop Hermes from divulging the identities of their father's enemies.

"Shall we do it now?" he asked.

Athena took a deep breath and slowly exhaled. "I'm ready when you are."

When they reached the dungeon beneath their father's throne, Athena was overwhelmed by memories of her first day, centuries ago, outside her father's belly, when Prometheus had first kissed her. Apollo sat on a bale of hay leaning against the dungeon wall with adamantine cuffs on his wrists. He looked up at them as they entered, his golden-brown hair falling into his otherwise bright eyes.

Hermes held up the caduceus. "I've come to put you into the deep boon of sleep, brother."

"What? Why?" the god of light asked as his eyelids began to droop.

"We've come to ask you about the rebellion against our father," Athena said, hoping to warn him, in case there was something he could do to prevent himself from telling all once they were inside the dream.

Hermes glanced at her suspiciously. "Good going, Athena. He would have had no memory of it. Now he can warn the others."

"How, when I'm a prisoner here?" Apollo pointed out.

"May I do it?" Athena asked, holding out her hand for the staff. She wanted to be able to wake Apollo the moment he began to reveal names.

Reluctantly, Hermes handed her the caduceus.

She moved closer to Apollo and put the staff against his chest. Suddenly, a bolt of electricity ran from Apollo, through the staff, and up her arm. She hadn't entered the dreamworld yet, but, nevertheless, a vision was playing out all around her, as if she were dreaming.

In the vision, she was lying on a bed in the captain's quarters of a ship. And Prometheus, holding the caduceus against her chest, stood over her.

"Hello, Athena."

"Prometheus? Is it really you?" she mumbled, confused.

"You know it is. For once, I was unable to elude your tenacious searching. Why won't you please give up?"

Of its own volition, her mouth moved. Words came of their own accord. "I need to know if you still love me."

"It's better you don't know. If I say yes, you'll long for what you cannot have. If I say no, you'll grow bitter and resentful."

Was she dreaming? What was happening?

"If you say no, I'll move on," she promised before she knew she was doing so.

Prometheus ran his fingers though his hair, wearing heartache on his face.

"But you can't, can you?" she insisted. "You're incapable of telling me a lie. Which means—"

Prometheus interrupted her speech by kissing her. His lips pressed softly at first, then harder and more passionately. With the staff of Hermes between them, he caressed her hair and spoke against her lips.

But wait, wasn't the staff against the chest of Apollo?

"I long for you every single day," Prometheus continued. "I try to distract myself from thoughts of you, but when I fail, I fail miserably."

She circled her arms around his neck, hardly able to believe what was happening.

"You stayed by my side for twenty years, enduring my torment with me," he said before kissing each of her cheeks. "Then you rescued me with the help of Heracles." He kissed her nose and chin.

Tears of joy and sorrow spilled from the corners of her eyes. "Why have you put us through this further agony of being separated? We could be together, making one another happy."

"I do not trust your father. The torment he put me through was unbearable. It haunts me still."

She kissed his furrowed brow. "I'm so sorry that I couldn't bear the burden for you."

"I couldn't risk him tormenting me further, and you right alongside me by associating with me, his number-one enemy. That's what he called me, did you know? His number-one enemy."

She pulled his head closer, so she could kiss him again. "Let me decide my own fate, will you? Let me choose which risks are worth taking."

He kissed her hair, her forehead, her neck, and then returned his mouth to hers. She held his curly hair in her fists, wanting to hold him there against her forever.

"I swore an oath," he reminded her. "I must help you in any way I can."

She stopped kissing him to study his face. "You don't help me by vanishing."

"It's better than the alternative."

"Prometheus—"

"You won't remember any of this when you wake," he said. "So shut up and kiss me for the few moments we have left."

His mouth pressed firmly against hers, sending waves of heat throughout her body. He lifted her head and pressed against her lips even harder, moving his tongue inside her mouth to sweep across her own.

"Oh, Prometheus," she whispered against his lips, her fingers digging into his biceps.

She moved her hands along his arms to his shoulders and then down his back, feeling every inch of him. Her fingers were both exploring and remembering.

As her hands moved down his back, a groan escaped from his throat, and he pressed his body hard against her, nearly driving the caduceus into her chest.

"Sweet Athena," he whispered.

In the bed, he rolled over, pulling Athena on top of him. His hands explored her backside, causing moans to escape her throat again and again. Then, he returned to their original position and said softly, "I could go on forever, but I fear you'll awake at any moment. I must leave before you do, so you have no memory of this encounter. It would only cause you heartache, as it will do me for all eternity. I will carry it around with me forever, Athena. I will treasure it for the both of us."

The vision ended abruptly. Athena blinked and assessed her surroundings. Apollo still lay asleep on the hay. Hermes stared at her wide-eyed.

Athena dropped the caduceus, unable to process what she had just experienced.

"So, that's what happened the last time you borrowed my staff?"

"You saw the vision, too?" she asked with trembling lips.

Hermes picked up his caduceus and took a few steps in her direction, so close that she could feel his breath on her face. "Tell me the truth, Athena. Have you seen Prometheus lately?"

"Yes," she admitted, not knowing what else to say.

"Do you know where he is?"

She shook her head. "But I might be able to lure him to us—if it's just you and me. I don't want anyone else to question him."

Hermes frowned. "Are you with him, then?"

"No. I'm trying to talk him out of his plans. He and my mother are working together. Oh, Hermes. It's breaking my heart." She fought tears. This wasn't a lie. She was confessing her true feelings.

Hermes took her into his arms. "My darling Athena. We'll sort this out together."

Alone in her bath, Athena leaned her head against the marble ledge and gazed up at the columns towering over her, wishing that, along with the week's grime from the battlefield in the desert, she could wash away the more pressing problems at home. She had told Hermes she would do her best to arrange a meeting between him and Prometheus, but how could she keep her word without endangering everyone she loved? Could Hermes be trusted not to organize an ambush on Prometheus? And conversely, could Prometheus?

Even worse, now that the dream she'd had on the ship with Prometheus had been restored to her memory, her desire to align herself with him and her mother was overpowering. To know that Prometheus had loved her so fiercely even then, years after his liberation by Heracles, made her feel less insecure about his feelings now. In her mother's cave, he'd claimed that he had never stopped loving her. That was easier to believe after seeing how fervently he'd loved her in the dream.

At least she'd convinced Hermes to abandon any further interrogation of Apollo until after the meeting with Prometheus. She wasn't sure how she'd managed that—or if she could trust Hermes not to do it without her later. She hadn't asked him to swear on the River Styx because of how it would look. For all she knew, Hermes could be with Apollo now doing the very thing she'd intended to do.

Athena groaned. There seemed to be no solution to her dilemma, no hope in sight. No matter what she chose to do, she would hurt people she loved. She supposed the only thing she could do was to choose the one she loved above all others.

Prometheus.

CHAPTER SEVENTEEN

The Point of No Return

Athena met her mother on the outskirts of her mother's cave and then followed her through the labyrinthine tunnel to her dwelling. To her disappointment, Prometheus was not there, but like always, a fire was dancing in the hearth. Athena sat on the couch across from it and told her mother what had happened—about wanting to interrogate Apollo, about the memory she received instead, and about Hermes's request for a meeting with Prometheus.

"I agreed to arrange it," Athena added.

"This is your chance to lure Hermes into a trap," her mother pointed out. "Will you swear your allegiance to me, your mother who loves you, and follow through with this plan?"

Athena had anticipated this. Hermes's request for a meeting with Prometheus had played right into her mother's hand. Had she or the Titan foreseen it?

"I will only swear my allegiance to Prometheus," Athena said. "I trust him above all others."

Although Metis appeared hurt, she nodded. "I understand."

Prometheus appeared from the twisting tunnels at the back of the dwelling. Had he been listening from the shadows?

He knelt before Athena, placing his hands on her waist. "My prayers to the Fates have been answered."

"You know they don't control our actions. They merely foresee them," Athena reminded him.

"Yes, but praying is a comfort when there's nothing else to be done."

Athena understood the feeling. In a more tender voice, she said, "I wish you would have let me keep the memory of our dream together."

"I feared it would be too great a burden for you. It was nearly too great a burden for me."

"You need to have more faith in me."

"I have great faith in you. But my instinct is to protect your heart."

She cupped his face. "Prometheus, I want to swear my allegiance to you, I really do, but I don't think it's wise. Can you trust that I'm on your side by my word alone?"

"I do trust your word, Athena, but why won't you swear?"

"I want to keep an eye on my father and those loyal to him. But if they suspect me, as I'm sure Hermes must, they'll interrogate me. I need to be able to swear that I have not sworn myself to you. Don't you see?"

"Yes. I see. You are wise, indeed, my love." He kissed her, sending rays of comforting warmth throughout her chest. It was a relief to have finally decided. There was no turning back now, even if she hadn't sworn.

"Return to my chamber with me tonight," he said gently. "We'll talk more about our conspiratorial plans tomorrow. Let's enjoy a blissful reunion first."

Athena's smile widened. "Lead the way."

The next morning, as Athena lay beside Prometheus in his bed in the cabin of a ship, she stared at the ceiling in a state of disbelief. After all these centuries, had they truly reunited? Or was she having an elaborate dream?

She looked over at the Titan, who still lay sleeping, and was tempted to run her fingers through his long, curly hair, but didn't want to risk waking him. She wished to study him for a bit longer, to take in his beauty and the wonder of this moment.

Tears welled in her eyes as she considered how she'd suffered without him for so very long. While it was true that she had led many men and women to greatness and had become a leader among the Olympians, her heart had never recovered from the loss of Prometheus. And, now that he was here lying beside her, it was difficult to believe it was more than a dream.

She had given him her word to support him. In doing so, she had declared herself an enemy of her father and of the other Olympians she knew were undoubtedly loyal to him: Ares, Hermes, Aphrodite, Hestia, and Demeter. And while she was in good company with Apollo and probably Artemis, what of Poseidon, Hades, and the others? Who were her enemies and who her friends?

Even more unsettling was the question of her mother and Prometheus's plans to overtake her father. When would those plans be revealed to her?

Her stomach twisted with worry and anxiety even as her heart bloomed with love and contentment.

Prometheus opened his eyes and held her gaze. "Good morning." He swept his lips across her cheek.

"Good morning." Could this really be her new reality? And could it become a regular occurrence?

"Did you sleep?" he asked as he smoothed her dark hair from her face.

"I did. I almost wonder if I'm sleeping still. This feels like a dream."

"I assure you it is not." He rested his weight on his elbows and looked down at her. "They can no longer call you the virgin goddess."

Athena rolled her eyes. "I never liked that moniker, anyway."

"But I know how you feel about it seeming unreal. I can hardly believe you are lying here beside me. It seems impossible."

"My stomach is in knots over what lies ahead," she confessed. "I need to know the plan."

"How would you like to meet your brother first?"

"Can I? Is it safe?"

"Are you hungry?"

"My stomach is too upset for food."

"Then, let's dress and go above deck. You'll find him in my captain's chair."

Athena's heart skipped a beat as she climbed out of bed and put a fresh shirt on beneath her breastplate. She wasn't sure how to feel. "Are there others on board? Other dissenters? You haven't told me who they are."

As Prometheus dressed, he said, "Helios and Selene are with us, and, as you know, Apollo and Artemis. We also have the support of Hades and the Underworld gods, including Hecate. Not Demeter. We don't have Poseidon yet, but we're working on it. Of course, we don't have Hera or Hestia or Ares, and probably never will. And as you know, Hermes, Aphrodite, and Hephaestus are still loyal to your father, but there's hope of converting them before a battle breaks."

She stepped into a clean skirt before securing her armored girdle. "All of the Underworld gods?"

"Yes, even Charon."

Athena was impressed. "How?"

"It's a long story, and your brother is anxious to meet you."

"Don't let on that you've recruited me just yet," Athena said. "In case my father has spies."

"As you wish." He slipped on his deck shoes and kissed her cheek.

"I'm worried Hermes may have followed me. He would understand a love affair, but not treason."

"Wise as always, Athena. We will keep your commitment to me under wraps. I've communicated your wishes to the others telepathically."

"Thank you." She conjured her boots and the rest of her armor into place—all save her helmet.

"And you'll find no other dissenters on board. Just Poros, my crew of two Korean orphans, and the twins of Thanatos."

"The twins of Thanatos?" Athena covered her mouth as her heart dropped. "Zeus knows where you are. He's been following them, knowing they'd lead him to you."

"The ship is warded, and we are in nearly constant motion. We've been very careful."

Her fear that spies would be watching multiplied. "Zeus will have eyes on the twins regardless. We must assume that they're being watched."

"We are careful on the open deck for that very reason."

"You go up first," she insisted. "I don't want them to know that I slept here last night."

"I have a feeling they know already," Prometheus said with a grin. "They *are* gods—even if they are children."

"The orphans, too?" Athena asked with wide eyes.

"No."

"Well, let's pretend for the spies, then," she insisted. "I'll leave and appear to be arriving for the first time."

He kissed her on the cheek before exiting the cabin.

Athena god-traveled to her chambers on Mount Olympus. She went to the mirror over her face-washing basin and stared at her reflection. "You can do this," she whispered. It wasn't her abilities she doubted; it was her course of action. She continued to fear that overthrowing her father was not the right course of action to take, but there was no changing it now.

She god-traveled to the sky above Prometheus's ship in the Arabian Sea. From the letters painted along the side of the bow, she learned it was called the *Marcella*. As she descended to the deck, she wondered why. Had Prometheus once loved a woman named Marcella?

Standing on the flybridge—the uppermost deck of the ship— were a group of teens and Prometheus. Two of the teens were obviously the children of Thanatos because they resembled their parents. The boy had dark, wavy hair and bright, blue eyes like his father. The girl had vibrant red hair and green eyes like her mother. The orphans from Korea also appeared to be siblings, having the same facial features and build. In the center of this group was a tall, sandy-haired boy with pale skin and stunning gray eyes—eyes that looked exactly like hers.

"Poros?" she asked.

"Hello, Athena," Poros said. "It's nice to finally meet you."

"Likewise." Athena glanced at the twins of Thanatos. "These children are gods. How is that possible?"

The last time she had seen them, they were demigods.

Poros was about to answer, but Prometheus interrupted him. "We have our ways."

"It's against Zeus's decree," Athena said sharply.

"And we are at war," Prometheus pointed out.

After staring at Poros for a few more moments in awkward silence, Athena turned to Prometheus. "Thank you for arranging this meeting, though I wonder why it didn't happen years ago."

Prometheus cleared his throat before saying, "Your brother has something to give you, don't you, Poros?"

Poros conjured a shield. Athena immediately recognized it as hers. It had been lost for sixteen years. Now she knew why.

"Your shield," Poros said, presenting it to Athena. "I believe our mother took it from you when she was pregnant with me. I'd like to give it back."

Athena studied her brother for a moment. She could hardly believe that he really existed. They, alone, shared the same mother and father. He looked so young and eager—hopeful, even. He had a gentleness about him, despite his obvious strength, that reminded her of Prometheus. The boy's smile was warm and compassionate like the Titan's. She wanted to hug him, to muss up his hair, but she couldn't dare appear to be sympathetic to her father's new number-one enemy, so she kept her distance.

She turned the shield over in her hands. "I wondered where it had gone. I tried to conjure it many times, unsuccessfully. Did our mother ever say why she stole it from me?"

Her mother emerged from the water and hovered above the sea about twenty yards away from the stern of the ship. Athena hadn't expected to see her here today. Was this even safe? Why would she risk exposure knowing Hermes could be spying on them?

Metis was dripping with sea water and surrounded by her purple aura. Two other goddesses were in the sea below, one silver and the other gold. They were her sisters: Prometheus's mother, Clymene, and Dione—Aphrodite's mother.

Athena hadn't seen Clymene in ages. She resisted the urge to embrace her. Instead, she pretended that it was *her* mother that she hadn't seen in ages.

"Mother!" Athena cried. "Is it really you?"

"I took your shield because I wanted something of yours to remember you by," her mother said. "Will you forgive me?"

"Where have you been?" Athena asked, throwing herself into the act of appearing shocked. "Why did you abandon me? For centuries, I begged my father to release you, and not long after I'd finally succeeded in getting you free, you left! Don't you care about me?"

Although Athena had already discussed this with her mother, she still wondered about the answer. Why hadn't her mother made any attempt to contact her in sixteen years?

"I care very much," Metis said, still hovering over the sea, which was beginning to swell. "But I sacrificed my desire to be with you for a higher purpose."

Athena glanced at Poros with a tinge of jealousy. "You've made that very clear."

"Please hear your mother out," Prometheus suggested. "She doesn't love your brother more than you."

"You can't speak for her," Athena said. "And you have no right to make excuses for her when you have none of your own."

"This isn't about love," Metis declared. "I love you and your brother equally. This is about justice and wisdom, things your father cares little about."

Athena gawked, imagining what Hermes would think. "Wisdom? How is yet one more son overthrowing his father an instance of wisdom? Why exchange one power-monger for another when history shows us that this is as good as it gets?"

"I'm not a power-monger," Poros insisted. "I don't want to rule the gods."

Athena turned back to her mild-mannered brother. "Then what do you want?"

"A better world," Poros said.

Athena wasn't sure how, but she believed him. He was just like Prometheus. The Titan had taught the boy well.

"Then why not appeal to our father?" Athena asked. "Why wage war?"

"Because if history has shown us anything," Metis said, "it's that your father will never change. He cannot be the one to lead us."

"Then who can?" Athena scoffed. "Prometheus?"

"I don't want to lead, either," Prometheus said gently.

She'd already known Prometheus didn't wish to rule, but she'd wanted Hermes to hear it. "Then who?" She regretted the question the moment it slipped through her lips.

"Why not *you*?" Metis implored her.

Oh, no, Athena thought. This was not the message she wanted to get back to Mount Olympus. She prayed to her mother to stop that kind of talk as she said, "You want me to overthrow my own father? Never."

"We want the gods to vote on a leader, as they do in most of the countries of the modern world," Poros explained.

"Why should the gods follow the lead of mortals?" Athena asked.

"Because, regardless of its origins, democracy is wise," her mother said. "And you know this to be true. Why are you fighting it?"

Athena blinked and shook her head, reminding her mother telepathically of the likelihood of spies.

"Take some time to think about it, Athena," Prometheus said. "Please?"

"You have no right to ask anything of me after what you did to me," Athena said, acting as if she were still angry with him—and if she was honest with herself, she was. "Neither of you do," she added, glaring at her mother. "Both of you abandoned me when I needed you, but my father has been at my side. Why should I turn my back on the one who has never left me?"

"He turned you to stone," Metis reminded her. "He convinced Poseidon to take you as a prisoner."

She was right, but that was water under the bridge. She'd been fighting with her father for her mother's release.

"Because he knew I wanted to release you," Athena said. "And now I understand why he resisted me."

Without another word, Athena god-traveled back to Mount Olympus. She was anxious for more details about the plan, but not out in the open. She prayed to Prometheus and her mother to meet her back at her mother's cave across the sea.

Don't risk god-travel, she warned them. *If Hermes is watching, he'll trace you to the cave. Fly around the world a few times in separate directions before meeting me there later tonight.*

We know what to do, her mother assured her.

CHAPTER EIGHTEEN

A Trap

The next morning, Athena looked for Hermes on Mount Olympus. When she didn't find him, she turned to Ares, who was sharpening his blade.

"Have you seen Hermes?"

"He's in the dungeon interrogating Apollo."

Athena's heart skipped a beat. Was Hermes using his caduceus on the god of light?

She flew down the dungeon steps and stopped outside the cell door. "Hermes?"

The face of the messenger god appeared at the barred window. "Has something happened?"

"I wondered if you might go swimming with me today."

His face paled, but he said, "I could use a break. Let's go."

As Hermes opened the door to exit, she caught a glance at Apollo, who sat on the bale of hay wearing the adamantine cuffs. He also wore a look of fear. Athena's stomach lurched as she wished she could communicate with him telepathically.

"Follow me," Hermes said.

They flew from the gates and over the open sea, where Helios was rising from the east.

"Is it safe to talk to you?" Athena asked.

"It depends on what you have to say."

"Oh, Hermes. Prometheus asked me to swear my allegiance to him. I couldn't do it. I love him, but I also love my father." What she was saying was not exactly a lie.

"Can't he and your mother be persuaded to stop this nonsense?"

"That's my hope."

He led her to their favorite stream on Mount Kithairon.

"Listen, darling Athena," he said once they were standing on the bank. "Whatever you do, don't play both sides. I've been guilty of that myself, and it's a miserable position to find yourself in."

Athena couldn't prevent the blush from crossing her face. "That's not my intention. I want to do what's right."

"I believe you. Were you able to arrange a meeting for me with Prometheus?"

She wringed her hands, considering several strategies before settling on the truth. "Hermes, he's agreed to meet you, but I fear it might be a trap. I can't guarantee your safety."

"I wouldn't expect otherwise. This is a risky business, to be sure. When and where will we meet?"

"He's waiting for us in the Minotaur's labyrinth."

When they arrived together on the island of Crete at the entrance to the labyrinth, Athena shuddered at the memory of Theseus taking the Minotaur's head centuries ago. What none of them knew at the time was that Poseidon had convinced Zeus to grant the creature immortality. Because of her role in the monster's suffering, Athena had steered clear of his domain. But last night, Metis and Prometheus had insisted that it was the perfect place to lure Hermes into their trap.

She led the way inside the cave, all the while praying to Prometheus. She had no idea which of the many twisting tunnels she was meant to take. *Prometheus, show me the way.*

Centuries ago, the labyrinth was designed by the craftsman Daedalus at the command of King Minos to imprison the Minotaur beneath the palace. It was an intricate and perplexing structure, making it nearly impossible for anyone trapped inside to find their way out. It was heavily warded, too, so that even most gods could not god-travel out of it.

Today, centuries later, the Knossos palace lay in ruins and was a site for tourists to visit, but the labyrinth below it was still intact and visible to those aware of its secret entrance.

"How far in must we go?" Hermes wanted to know. "This should be sufficient for any protective wards to prevent us from being overheard."

"I agree." Then aloud, she called, "Prometheus? Are you here?"

Her voice echoed off the stone walls, punctuated by the drip from a nearby water source.

Something slithered past her boot. It was a snake. She watched it flee into the crevices of the cavern wall. Other critters fled, too: a rat, a family of spiders, and a pair of mice.

The hair on the back of her neck stood on end.

From behind them near the entrance came a loud hiss. She turned back to see the monster Echidna—the half-woman, half-snake—slithering toward them.

Athena conjured her spear, ready to fight, but Hermes pointed to something creeping toward them from another tunnel. From the shadows emerged Chimera—the monster with the heads of a lion, a goat, and a serpent.

Athena's mind raced as she calculated their next move, her thoughts sharp and clear even amidst the danger surrounding them.

"Run!" Hermes shouted, leaving her in his dust.

Not wanting to get separated, she flew after him with both monsters fast on her heels, every turn of the tunnels leading them deeper into the maze's suffocating embrace.

"Prometheus!" she shouted at the top of her lungs.

Had the beasts thwarted Prometheus's plan? Or had he arranged for them to be there?

Talk to me, she urged the Titan telepathically.

But she got no reply.

She struggled to keep the swift messenger god in sight, following the same twists and turns he made, not wanting to lose him. She felt the cold sting of a serpent's tongue slap her thigh. She shook it loose and flew higher, near the top of the cavern ceiling, dodging the uneven stones lodged in the cavern walls.

Echidna's tail whipped around one of Athena's ankles and tugged her back, but Athena quickly used her dagger to stab it away before recovering and continuing down the passageway. When the tunnel narrowed, she slid against the sometimes ragged, sometimes smooth stone of the walls, chafing and burning her flesh on her exposed arms and thighs.

Hermes suddenly dove into a tight nook at the end of a tunnel, so she dove in after him, bumping her head against his knee. She reduced her size, to make more room—just as she used to do when she was trapped inside her father. Fortunately, monsters did not share this power, so when the two beasts reached the nook, they shrieked and hissed and clawed at it, trying to get at the gods inside.

"You can't hide in there forever," Echidna hissed.

"It's impossible to god-travel out of here," Hermes said to Athena as he panted for air. "We're trapped."

"Not if I can help it." Athena hurled her spear at the snake woman. The weapon began small in Athena's hand, but as it left the protective nook, it enlarged to its natural size and pierced the monster in the throat, knocking it over. The serpentine tail flailed wildly as Echidna screamed in pain.

The other beast barreled toward them just as the duo were attempting their escape.

Athena pulled her spear from Echidna's neck, but the writhing tail found the goddess and began to coil itself around her, suffocating her.

Hermes flung his golden blade at Chimera's lion head, nearly decapitating it. The beast wailed and growled in torment. Then the messenger god retrieved the blade and cut Athena free from Echidna's coiled tail as he dodged Chimera's blows.

"This way," Hermes cried, grabbing Athena's hand.

Before they had gotten very far, the Minotaur appeared, glowering angrily down at them. "You shall not pass this way!"

"Asterion?" Hermes shouted with surprise.

The monster had the body of a man and the head of a bull, and his eyes were fierce, his teeth sharp.

"Come on," Athena led Hermes away from the beast down another corridor.

Yet another monster emerged from the darkness, and with a loud shriek, blocked their passage. It was Scylla, her six heads towering over them as she shimmied on eight tentacles. A mass of snarling wolves grew from her waist, snapping their fierce teeth.

Athena drove her spear into Scylla, but it had little impact on the monster except to make her angrier.

Narrowly evading tentacles and claws, Athena retrieved her spear from the belly of the beast and was about to attack again when Hermes grabbed her hand and shouted, "This way!"

He led her down yet another serpentine path that came to a fork.

Noticing a light at the end of the tunnel to their right, Athena tugged Hermes in that direction. "Over here!"

She could hear Scylla tumbling along behind them. The injury from Athena's spear must have slowed the beast down.

The tunnel soon opened into a large chamber filled with water. Light from Helios poured in through a crack in the ceiling and reflected on the surface of the pool.

"There's our way out," Athena said, pointing to the crack.

Before either she or Hermes could make a move, the ground shuddered beneath them, and something enormous sent bubbles to the surface of the pool. As the gods flew toward the ceiling, the monstrous head of the Hydra emerged from the water and blocked their path. The entire cavern trembled. Eight necks, severed from their heads by Heracles centuries ago, hung limp at the beast's sides. But the one immortal head in the center was ferocious enough, especially with the help of Hydra's claws and powerful tail.

The monster was covered in green scales. Her one head was mostly a wide snout with several rows of sharp teeth. A forked tongue darted out like a frog's, threatening to snatch Athena up with each lash.

As Athena was about to throw her spear, Hermes grabbed her hand and tugged her to their right through a tiny opening that required them to reduce themselves in size. Traveling through such a small crevice was risky when there was no light in sight, because it could be a dead end and another trap. Athena was relieved when it opened into another chamber strangely filled with wooden chairs and a golden cage.

Before she knew it was happening, an unseen force took ahold of her and pushed her into the golden cage, along with Hermes. The door slammed shut.

Too late, Athena realized that she and Hermes had been corralled to the cage by the monsters.

"It's adamantine," Hermes groaned, referring to what she'd mistaken as gold.

"Reveal yourself," she shouted into the darkness. She expected to see Phorcys or Keto, the parents of the monsters, removing the helm of invisibility, which they must have stolen from Hades, thwarting her mother and Prometheus's plan to trap Hermes.

She gasped when the helm came off, and the person who'd been wearing it was Prometheus.

So, the Titan *had* orchestrated the trap with the monsters.

"Prometheus?" She was truly astonished that he had allowed her to be in such danger.

"I thought you were committed to me," Prometheus said to Athena. His voice wasn't angry—but hurt. "You don't think I have spies, too? I know what you said to Hermes. I know everything."

Athena's eyes widened, unsure whether what was unfolding before her was the expression of genuine feelings of betrayal or merely an act for Hermes's benefit.

"I didn't swear," she reminded him.

"And now I know why," Prometheus said bitterly. "But it's Hermes I want to talk to." The Titan turned to the messenger god as Athena tried to process what was happening. "There are things you need to know about your father that would make your skin crawl."

"I doubt that," the messenger god said.

Before Prometheus could say more, he frowned at Hermes. "I just got word that the *Marcella* is under attack."

Prometheus vanished, leaving Athena and Hermes alone in their prison.

It suddenly dawned on Athena that Hermes had been distracting her and Prometheus while the other Olympians had gone to attack her brother. She inwardly berated herself for not anticipating this move.

Then, she whipped around to glare at Hermes. "What do they intend to do with Poros?"

She'd only just met the boy, but she loved him. He was her brother.

"My orders were to create a diversion," Hermes replied. "I know nothing more, though I imagine Zeus will put Poros into the Titan Pit or swallow him, as he did your mother."

"But he's so young," she said of her brother. "Only fifteen years old."

"You were fighting Giants at a younger age."

"I was born ready. He doesn't have that fighting spirit. Have you seen him?"

Hermes frowned. "Yes. He seems like a fine boy, Athena. I'm truly sorry."

"Doesn't it bother you that a father will destroy a son? Zeus was even willing to sacrifice you, was he not?"

"We had no way of knowing that your lover had recruited the monsters."

"Even so, Zeus asked you to take a risk on his behalf. Hermes, it should be the other way around. Fathers are meant to protect their children."

"It sounds like you haven't been honest with me. Are you not a loyal daughter? Did you lure me here?"

How could she be a loyal daughter when her parents were at odds with one another?

"I told you it might be a trap," she reminded him. "I don't know what to think. I can't believe Prometheus put us in such danger."

"Maybe the monsters weren't meant to eat us. Maybe they were only meant to corral us to this cage."

She supposed he was right. "I don't like the way any of them are behaving—not my father, not my mother, and not even Prometheus."

"Are you meant to recruit me?" Hermes asked. "Is that your role in all of this?"

She shook her head. "I know that to be impossible. I think we're meant to be leverage for a prisoner exchange with Apollo."

Hermes belted a sardonic laugh. "That's not happening."

"Tell me about it."

Less than a minute had passed when Apollo entered with his sister on his heels.

"Apollo?" Hermes cried. "Is it really you?"

"You're free to go," he said, brandishing the key.

As Apollo unlocked the cage, Athena stared at him and Artemis with wide eyes. "What's happened?"

Artemis was the one who answered, "Prometheus sacrificed himself to save your brother. He gave himself up and agreed to free you in exchange for Apollo."

"What?" Athena was struggling to comprehend, to imagine how it had played out.

"But Poros is far from safe," Apollo warned. "You can be sure that another attack by the loyalists is forthcoming."

CHAPTER NINETEEN

Return Trip

T ell me what happened," Athena demanded as she and Hermes stepped from their adamantine prison. "I need the details."

"Asterion?" Hermes said with surprise when the Minotaur emerged from the shadows.

The monster did not appear threatening or menacing when he said, "I'm here to guide you out."

"Where are the other monsters?" Athena asked.

The Minotaur frowned. "They've returned to the sea. Follow me."

Athena decided to trust him, seeing no reason for the half-man, half-bull to betray them. As they followed him, she turned to Apollo and Artemis. "You may as well tell all."

"Zeus is determined to swallow Poros," Apollo replied as they turned down another corridor. "He launched an attack on Prometheus's ship while Hermes created a diversion."

"I worked out that part." Athena gave Hermes a look of reproach. "Was anyone injured beyond repair? Are the children okay?"

"The mortal children—the Korean orphans—are safe in Tartarus," Artemis explained, ducking when the tunnel narrowed. "Not dead, just being protected by the Furies for as long as the ship is in danger."

"The Underworld gods are on the side of the rebellion?" Hermes asked. "I wondered. All?"

"We're not at liberty to say," Apollo demurred.

"There's water ahead," the Minotaur warned just before he leapt over it.

The gods flew after him.

"But Poros and the children of Thanatos are safe?" Athena asked once they were on the other side of the pool.

"Their parents, your mother, and her sisters are protecting them," Artemis assured her.

Athena was relieved that there had been no casualties.

"We were at a standstill," Artemis continued as they rounded another bend. "Hades was beneath the helm when he appeared with a blade at Zeus's neck, but Ares had his blade on Poros."

"Oh," Hermes muttered as he shook his head.

Artemis added, "Hades offered to relinquish Zeus for Poros, but Zeus wouldn't have it. He kept stalling. We feared he had an ace up his sleeve, that something was coming. That's when Prometheus began negotiating. He would take Poros's place if Apollo could be traded for the two of you. Zeus jumped on it."

"I was no good to him anyway," Apollo pointed out, "though I did fear torture was in my future."

"I wouldn't put it past our father," Artemis said sardonically as they flew over another pool of water.

Athena shuddered. "Tell me he's put Prometheus in his dungeon and not in the Titan Pit."

"Worse, I'm afraid," Apollo said.

Artemis and Apollo exchanged somber glances.

"Tell me," Athena insisted.

Apollo sighed. "As we speak, Zeus is chaining Prometheus to the summit of Mount Ida to endure his old punishment again."

Athena gasped and stared at the god of light and music as if he had grown two more heads. "That can't be! Please say it isn't so!"

"The Titan is doing it for you," Artemis said. "He says you are the future."

Reeling with the news, heart racing, throat tight, and barely able to breathe, Athena touched the Minotaur's humanoid hand. "Please, get me out of here as fast as you can."

The Minotaur began to run. The gods quickly flew after him, twisting and turning with the winding corridors of the maze.

Once free of the labyrinth, Athena frantically flew west to the center of Crete, to the peak of Mount Ida, where Prometheus already lay on his rock in chains.

"This can't be happening!" Athena called to the Titan as she flew to his side. "Tell me I'm dreaming—in a nightmare!"

"Sweet Athena, you're in danger here. You don't want to be seen by my side."

"I don't care anymore." Tears streamed down her cheeks. "Oh, darling, I can't bear this again."

He gave her a somber smile. "If I can, you can."

Artemis and Apollo caught up to her. Hermes wasn't with them.

"We'll do what we can to help you escape," Artemis promised. "We wondered if this key to the cage might work."

Hopeful, Athena eagerly snatched the key from Artemis and quickly pressed it into the lock, but it didn't fit.

"It was worth the try," Apollo mused as he took the key from Athena. "We'll keep searching for it. Hades has agreed to loan us the helm."

"Thank him for me," Prometheus said.

The twins nodded forlornly and disappeared.

Athena knelt beside her lover and combed his long hair from his face, trying to comfort him as best as she could. "I heard what you did for Poros."

"I bought him more time, that's all. The rebellion will need to protect him and act soon."

Athena supposed it was time to accept that the revolution was really happening. The attempt to unseat her father was at hand.

She touched his cheek. "What you said in the Minotaur's labyrinth—"

"An act for Hermes, nothing more."

Relief swept through Athena as she buried her face in Prometheus's neck. "Oh, thank goodness. I swear now on the River Styx to always be loyal to you."

"We probably don't have much time together. I'm sure someone from Zeus's army will return to spy on me, and if they find you here—"

"Like I said, I don't care anymore."

"Don't say that. I care. It would break my heart to see you captured—or worse."

"Shut up and kiss me," she pleaded, cupping his face. The cuffs on his wrists prevented him from embracing her, but he touched her face, pushed a strand of hair behind her ear, and kissed her.

Love soared through Athena, through every inch of her body, sending a rush of euphoria through her despite the suffering that lay ahead.

Suddenly, Prometheus chuckled, as if he, too, were alight with joy.

She looked down at him, perplexed. Why should they be laughing with the sun so close to setting?

"Remember that first day in your father's dungeon? Remember how we passed the week together?" he asked tenderly.

She grinned. "How could I forget?"

"We barely knew each other then," he pointed out.

"You swore on the River Styx to always help me," she reminded him. "When I pointed out that you barely knew me, you said that—"

"I knew all I needed to."

She kissed him again, holding him close, but not without noticing that Helios was preparing to make his descent. It would soon be time.

Athena could not allow him to endure his old punishment again, especially when his crime had been to protect her brother. Without warning him, she shielded the Titan's body with her own and clung to him—her arms wrapped around his neck and her legs wrapped around his like a vice, to prevent him from pushing her off.

"What are you doing?" he asked, his voice full of concern. "Athena, get off, get out of the way."

"When will you ever learn that you can't tell me what to do?" she whispered in his ear.

She recognized the thick anxiety that hung in the air, palpable and suffocating, as the light changed with the setting sun. She felt Prometheus stiffen beneath her—a reflex his body must have never unlearned.

Then she buried her face in his neck just as the flapping of the eagle's wings could be heard overhead. She steeled herself by gritting her teeth and clinging to her love. She hoped the bird would mistake her liver for the Titan's and spare him pain; however, even if the eagle plowed through her and into Prometheus, she hoped sharing the burden with him would still bring him solace.

The vicious beak tore through her side, ripping her flesh apart. She groaned into Prometheus's neck as he begged her to move, to spare herself, and then she gave into the pain and fainted.

When Athena awakened, night had fallen, and she felt rain dripping on her.

"Athena?" Prometheus asked from beneath her. "Are you awake?"

"I think so," she muttered. "What's happening?"

"The Nephelae are washing the blood from your body, and Aether is keeping the other predators away."

"Like in the old days," she said with a smirk, unable to move.

"Take it easy," Prometheus warned. "You're still healing."

"What about you?" she asked. "Were you spared?"

"I was. But I won't have you do that again."

"You are not the boss of me."

He laughed. "Don't I know it."

"Ow, that hurts. You're bouncing me around with your laughter."

"Sorry."

"I wish you could put your arms around me. I wish you could hold me."

"I do, too, sweet Athena. Believe me."

He kissed her nose. She lifted her chin and pressed her lips to his. The warmth from the kiss moved through her, like a healing balm that rejuvenated her weary body and reinvigorated her soul. She could feel her wounds healing as he stroked her cheek and caressed her lips with his.

The rain ceased, and without turning to look at them, Athena thanked the clouds for their kindness.

As she lay there on Prometheus with her face nestled in his neck, she heard the crickets singing and the wind blowing through the leaves. She could feel the warm beams of Selene on the back of her legs, and she had the urge to turn around and look up at the stars. Every move she made hurt, but she was determined. Prometheus readjusted to accommodate her new position, cradling her as best he could beneath the heavens.

They lay there searching for the constellations together for many quiet minutes before Athena said, "If I could be with you like this every day and every night, I could get used to the eagle."

"Don't say that. I don't want you to get used to it."

"I didn't mean to make light of the decades you endured it."

"I know, but I want more for you. I see more for you."

Suddenly, Prometheus's cuffs were unlocked.

"What's this?" the Titan whispered with surprise.

It's Artemis, Artemis said to Athena telepathically. Athena soon realized the goddess was beneath the helm of invisibility. *Hermes gave me the key. He said that Hera knows you're pregnant. Hermes asked me to beg you to hide until the conflict is over, for the sake of your child if not your own.*

Athena gawked. She was pregnant? How was that possible? Hadn't Hera rendered all deities infertile? Her mind reeled.

With his hands free, Prometheus cupped her belly, bringing her back to her senses and making it apparent that Artemis was communicating with him, too.

Artemis, Athena prayed. *The eagle . . . I placed myself—my child—in harm's way to protect Prometheus. Can you tell if the baby is still alive?*

Athena had learned from her mother that gods did not become immortal until after their birth. This meant that Athena's child had been vulnerable to the ravishes of the eagle.

I'll tell Apollo to meet you at your mother's cave. Go there now and take the helm.

Artemis lifted the helm from her head and placed it on Athena's before fleeing. Then, Prometheus swept Athena into his arms and took flight, too. He carried her over land and water to the Arabian Sea and her mother's secret cave. Athena did not see the *Marcella* where it had previously been anchored, but she waited until they were safely in her mother's warded dwelling before asking about it.

"It's been moved," he said as he gently laid her on her mother's couch. "And Poros and the other children are under Hades's protection. My gods, Athena, I had no idea you were with child."

"Obviously, neither did I. And after that eagle had me for dinner, I may no longer be. Oh, Prometheus!" She threw her arms around his neck and prayed to the Fates to please let her baby be alive, even though she knew they had no power to help her.

CHAPTER TWENTY

Mothers

A thena buried her face in Prometheus's chest and prayed to Metis. For the first time since she'd sprung from her father's head, Athena needed her mother.

"Someone is coming," Prometheus said as he climbed to his feet.

Apollo appeared in the entryway.

Both relieved and disappointed—for she'd half-expected the arrival of her mother—Athena asked him, "How can I be pregnant?"

"I'm not sure," the god of music and healing replied. "Perhaps Hera didn't think it was necessary to bother with you or Artemis or Hestia because—"

"Because we're the virgin goddesses." Athena's tone was filled with sarcasm. She hated that the virginity of females had been so highly revered by humans while the virginity of males had not. Males seemed to be more admired for their sexual prowess. It wasn't just the double standard that irked her. She wanted to be revered for her leadership, her wisdom, her battle skills, and her other talents—not whether she'd lain with someone.

Apollo nodded. "And Prometheus was nowhere to be found—though I don't believe she did anything to the male deities, only the female."

"Can you tell us if the baby survived the eagle?" Prometheus wanted to know.

"Remove your armor," Apollo instructed Athena.

When Athena moved, the pain was excruciating, and she groaned involuntarily.

"Let me help," Prometheus offered.

Apollo studied Athena's abdomen. After many minutes, he said, "I'm afraid your uterus was ruptured by the bird, and the embryo, while still living, is ectopic."

"What does that mean?" Athena wanted to know.

"The child was dislodged." Apollo crossed his arms. "It can't survive if it's not implanted in the womb. I'm sorry, Athena."

Athena furrowed her brow. "Can you move it back to where it belongs?"

"What?" Apollo laughed nervously. "I'd have to cut you open again—to basically inflict the same damage that you just suffered from the eagle."

Prometheus kneeled at her side. "You've been through so much already."

"I want this child, our child, to live," Athena insisted. "I can handle the pain." She looked up at Apollo. "Or maybe there's something you can give me for that, some modern medicine?"

"There are more things to consider than whether you experience pain," Apollo pointed out.

"Like what?" Prometheus squeezed Athena's hand as he looked up at Apollo with worry lines across his forehead.

"You recall how Hephaestus was never able to recover after Hera threw him from Mount Olympus as an infant? He suffered terrible damage and even death. And when his immortal soul returned to his body, well, you know how the story ends."

Hephaestus even today had a hunchback and a limp.

"Why are you telling us this?" Athena asked. "Are you saying that our baby may never recover from the trauma it has already endured?"

"Yes. If it survives at all, it may be severely deformed—monstrous even."

Athena covered her mouth and met Prometheus's worried gaze.

He tenderly kissed the top of her head. "Sweet Athena. Perhaps it wasn't meant to be."

She shook her head. "I don't care if it's monstrous. This is our child. I want to do everything possible to help it to live. Don't you?"

Prometheus stroked her cheek. "Yes, but you're the one who must endure the pain, so it should be your choice."

She turned to Apollo with tears in her eyes. "Can you see anything in the future? Anything at all?"

"I see you as the leader of the Olympians. I see you and Prometheus together. But I cannot see a child."

"Only the Fates know for certain what the future holds." Athena gripped Apollo's arms. "Please help me, brother."

Apollo sighed. "If that's what you want, we must act immediately."

Athena closed her eyes and prayed again to her mother. "It's what I want."

"We could really use your help—and by we, I mean the revolution," Apollo objected. "Is the life of this child, who may turn out to be deformed and weak if it survives at all, worth keeping you out of service to the cause? We need you." Apollo glared at Prometheus. "We need both of you."

Athena stared blankly at Apollo with an open mouth, not sure how to reply. Was he really suggesting that she was being selfish by putting her child first?

Prometheus covered his face with his hands. Athena had the feeling he was praying to his mother.

Before Athena could think of what to say, her mother appeared and addressed Apollo, "The point of this revolution is to protect individual liberties, not to sacrifice them."

"You sacrificed," Apollo argued.

"By choice," Metis shot back. "Athena alone must make this choice, and we will respect it."

Athena wiped her eyes and smiled at her mother, feeling both surprised and pleased that she had come to defend her.

"Should Athena choose to put her child first," Metis continued, "I'll remain by her side so that Prometheus can fight in my place, for he is much stronger than I."

Prometheus cupped Athena's face. "Tell me what you want, my love."

"I want you to fight for the cause while I fight for our child."

He kissed her tenderly on the forehead. "It's hard to leave you like this, but I'm relieved to hear you say that. I'll return to check on you as often as I can." He turned to Apollo. "Do you need anything for the surgery? Medicine?"

"I can conjure what I need," Apollo assured him. "Go to Hades if you're ready to serve, and you'd better use the helm."

To both Apollo and Metis, Prometheus said, "I leave her in your hands." Then he kissed Athena again and disappeared.

Athena prayed for Prometheus's safe return. She prayed to Clymene and to Hades and begged them to watch the Titan's back.

While Apollo prepared his instruments and medicines, Metis took a washcloth to Athena's abdomen.

"My darling daughter," she said gently. "I'm sorry for your suffering."

"Thank you, Mother," Athena replied. "I'm so grateful that you're here with me."

"We're back to where we started, eh?" Metis said with a laugh. "Imprisoned together and worried about birth?"

"I think fondly of those days."

"I'm glad to hear you say so."

Apollo leaned over Athena with a needle and syringe. "This is for the pain," he said before he stabbed her in the belly. "It won't put you to sleep but should numb the nerves."

"Why not put her to sleep?" Metis asked.

"We don't know what to expect from the embryo of gods. They aren't immortal, but they grow rapidly and have power. She needs to be awake in case a decision needs to be made."

Metis frowned.

"I want to be awake," Athena said. "I'm frightened for the child, but I'm otherwise strong and unafraid."

Metis smiled down at her and stroked Athena's hair. "You've been that way from the beginning—strong and unafraid."

"As have you, Mother."

"Can you feel this?" Apollo said as he poked her with a needle.

Athena shook her head.

"Then, I shall begin," the god said just before he took a scalpel to her flesh.

Athena gritted her teeth, hoping with all her might that the baby would be safely tucked back into her womb and allowed to flourish there. She'd never wanted something more desperately—except, perhaps, to find Prometheus.

"Shall I ask you a riddle to distract you?" Metis offered, still stroking Athena's hair.

"Yes, please."

"Okay, then. What breaks but never falls, and what falls but never breaks?"

Athena thought for a moment. "Day breaks but never falls. Night falls but never breaks. Come on, Mother. You'll have to do better than that."

Metis laughed. Athena tried not to notice the look of worry on Apollo's face as he performed his surgery. Even her mother had to struggle to keep the fear from her eyes.

"Fine," Metis said. "Here's another: What goes through cities and fields but never moves?"

Athena felt a sudden stab of pain and cried out.

Apollo gave her another injection.

"Is everything okay?" Athena asked.

"It just takes time," Apollo replied. "I must cut through several layers to find the embryo. I'm nearly there."

"A road," Athena said to her mother. "Do you have another?"

"One more," Metis said. "This one is the most difficult of all, I believe: What does man love more than life, hate more than death or mortal strife; that which contented men desire; the poor have, the rich require; the miser spends, the spendthrift saves, and all men carry to their graves?"

"Easy," Athena replied with a smile, feeling better now that the medicine had once again numbed the pain. "Nothing."

It took Apollo over an hour to finish the surgery and to stitch Athena back up. He'd successfully moved the embryo to Athena's womb, but its ability to grow and thrive was still unknown. He told Athena to lie as still as possible and to drink and eat as much as she could stomach.

"Sleep, too," he advised. "And call if you need me. I'm off to help the cause."

Athena took his hand and squeezed it. "Thank you, brother. I'll never forget this."

He gave her a solemn nod and disappeared.

Metis sat on the wooden chair close to the couch and stroked Athena's cheek. "Sleep now, my darling daughter. I will watch over you."

Grateful for her mother's presence during this time of severe anxiety and trepidation, Athena closed her eyes and prayed to Hypnos.

When Athena next awoke, the first thing she did was check her abdomen. The stitching had healed, and she was surprised to find that her usually flat stomach appeared to have a bump.

"Mother?" Athena looked around the cave.

"Oh, good, you're awake." Her mother entered and handed her a glass. "Drink this. It's water with the juice of a lemon. It should settle your stomach so we can get some food in you."

"Is this bump from swelling? Or is the baby truly growing?" Athena held her breath as she waited for her mother's answer.

"I wish I knew, my darling Athena. Can you feel any movement yet?"

"No, should I?"

"Not usually this soon, but every goddess's experience is different."

Athena drank the lemon water. Her stomach felt queasy, but the lemon seemed to help.

"I've made you some broth." Her mother handed her a golden goblet that was warm to the touch. "See if your stomach can handle it before trying solid food."

Athena sipped from the goblet. The broth tasted good and went down smoothly. "It's delicious. Thank you." Then she asked, "How long was I asleep?"

"Three days."

"Three days? Oh, my. I can't believe I lost three whole days."

"You needed the sleep to heal."

"Have you heard from Prometheus?"

"No, but I'm in nearly constant communication with Clymene. Poseidon joined the cause. With him on our side, the rebellion is planning to strike—that's all I know."

The news of an impending strike made Athena uneasy. "No idea how soon?"

"No. I'm sorry."

Athena reached out to Prometheus: *I slept for three days. I'm drinking and eating. I think the baby is growing. How are you? Please update me on the rebellion.*

Zeus locked Demeter and Iris in adamantine cages. He threatened to swallow Demeter and rip the wings from Iris.

Athena felt like a Giant had just sat on her chest. *But they're loyalists.*

And dearly loved by rebels. Zeus knows that Persephone and Hecate will do anything to save Demeter, and Morpheus—and by extension Hypnos and Hades—will do anything to spare Iris. Your father is desperate now that Poseidon has converted.

Athena was shocked to hear how far Zeus was willing to go to protect his throne—to use those most loyal to him as leverage. *How will the rebellion respond? What's the plan?*

We're working on it. Hecate channeled Demeter's power to take your form and voice and pretend to be you, to throw the loyalists off.

That's great news. I'll be sure to thank her.

I'll see if I can get away soon to be with you.

Be careful, she prayed.

Always.

I love you.

As do I you, my sweet Athena.

Athena turned to her mother. "Why didn't you tell me about Demeter and Iris?"

"Stress isn't good for the baby. Prometheus should know better."

"Leaving me in the dark is worse."

"I disagree, my darling. Now, try not to worry and see if you can eat this fish. The protein will be good for both you and the baby."

Twelve more days passed before Prometheus finally managed to return to Metis's cave.

"Sweet Athena." He knelt on the floor beside the couch and cupped her abdomen. "You've grown. Does this mean all is well?"

It was true. Athena's bump had doubled in size.

"There's no way of knowing," Metis warned from across the room where she was preparing a fish stew. "But we're hopeful."

"What's happening with the rebellion?" Athena asked.

"There's still nothing to report. Persephone seems to be arguing for a plan. I'll let you know the moment I know something. I promise. Now, tell me, how do you feel?"

"Anxious," she admitted. "Anxious about the rebellion, anxious about the baby. Oh, I hate not knowing what will be."

He kissed her cheeks, her forehead, her lips. "Apollo already told us that you will be the leader of the Olympians and that you and I will be together."

Athena had been about to say that that was no longer enough, but she bit her tongue.

Their conversation was interrupted by the arrival of Clymene.

"Mother?" Prometheus climbed to his feet. "Has something happened?"

"Hecate was traded for Demeter and Iris and is being forced to perform a location spell for Metis. She'll do her best to mislead them, but, just in case, we need to move Athena as soon as possible."

"Wouldn't it be better if I left the cave and lured the loyalists into a trap?" Metis suggested.

Clymene frowned. "Yes, except that we believe Prometheus may have been followed. If not him, me."

"How? I god-traveled," the Titan argued.

"Hermes stole the helm. We think someone's been infiltrating our camp. This is all speculation, but we need to be safe."

"But where will I go?" Athena sat up as slowly as she could, so as not to harm the baby.

"I have a plan," Clymene assured her. "I arranged for it the moment I heard you were here, as a backup."

Metis crossed the room and embraced her sister. "I can't thank you enough. I should have thought of a backup plan myself."

"Selene will come in her chariot as soon as night falls," Clymene explained. "She'll be shielded by the Nephelae. I'll be watching for her, and as soon as she approaches the mouth of this cave, I'll let you know. Prometheus, you'll need to quickly bring Athena to Selene's chariot."

"Then what?" Prometheus wanted to know.

"Selene will take Athena on her route around the world and then deliver her to her cave," Clymene said. "The loyalists have no idea that Selene and Helios are working with us, so Athena should be safe there—for a while, anyway."

"How long before nightfall?" Athena asked.

"Four more hours," Clymene replied.

"What if the loyalists attack before then?" Prometheus wondered as he glanced nervously at Athena.

"The rebellion will come to our defense," Metis said. "Won't they, sister?"

"Indeed. I'll keep watch and keep you posted."

"Oh, Clymene, thank you," Athena cried. "I can't thank you enough."

Clymene flew to Athena and kissed her cheek. "I've always liked you, dear. I love the way you love my son."

Athena smiled up at her as tears pooled in her eyes. "Thank you. That means the world to me."

CHAPTER TWENTY-ONE

Fathers

s Athena lay on her mother's couch in the secret cave on an island in the Arabian Sea, her mind churned with fear and worry for her unborn child. She had never intended to have children. First, she never believed she and Prometheus would one day reunite, and she could never have given her heart to another. Then, in recent years, at the command of Zeus and with the support of the Olympian council, Hera had supposedly rendered it impossible. Despite those things, she had never wanted to bring a child into a world full of pain and suffering. Amphisbaena had fulfilled her need to mother. But now that the child existed, Athena loved it more than she loved herself. Her love was as constant as her heartbeat and as profound as the connection between her body and her soul. She would do everything in her power to protect it.

She glanced at the opening of the chamber, half-expecting to see a loyalist lurking there.

The minutes seemed to drag by. For the twenty years she'd been at Prometheus's side awaiting the eagle, she had prayed for the delay of sunset, and now here she was wishing she could speed it along. If Zeus and his followers were to infiltrate her mother's cave before the arrival of her allies, there would be no hope.

"Should Apollo and Artemis come now, just to be safe?" Athena asked her mother and Prometheus.

"Clymene will let us know if she senses any sign of danger," Prometheus assured her. "Try not to worry. If our allies come too soon, they may needlessly give away our location."

"The opening of this cave system if difficult to find," her mother added. "That's why I chose it. It's why I met you outside the first few times you came."

Athena nodded, slowly exhaling, trying to keep her heartbeat steady. Despite their reassurances, she stole glances at the chamber entrance every few seconds.

Prometheus squeezed her hand. "Their fear of an ambush will keep them from entering."

Athena believed he was probably right, but she'd known her father to infiltrate caves against her advice in the past.

And, even if her father did not infiltrate, he would certainly be assembling an ambush of his own. The moment she emerged from the cave, he and his followers would attack. The Nephelae would have little hope of shielding her.

Athena turned to Prometheus. "Tell your mother to ask the Nephelae to come early and to encircle one of the nearby islands with a thick fog."

"To act as a decoy," he said with a nod. "Good idea."

"After they've attracted the attention of our enemies," Metis chimed in, "the clouds should gradually form a blanket over the entire Arabian Sea. We will still need that shield when Selene comes."

"A wise improvement to my plan," Athena acknowledged as she woefully cupped her abdomen.

Only a few more minutes had passed when Athena groaned. "One of you, please distract me. I need another riddle or something to help pass the time."

"Shall I tell you about your brother?" Prometheus offered.

Athena arched a brow. "You know him well, do you?"

"In a way, he's like a son to me. He came to me five years ago to train."

Metis crossed the room to the couch and sat on one end with Athena's feet in her lap. "Poros was anxious to leave this cave. For the first ten years of his life, he never left it—not once."

"He and I have a lot in common," Athena noted. "We were both born in a prison with our mother as our only company."

"And I was the first person you met on the outside," Prometheus pointed out.

Athena grinned, her memory of their week together in her father's dungeon providing her with a momentary reprieve from the stress and anxiety of the present.

"He used to entertain himself with stories," Metis said. "Although he was anxious to see the outside world, he never lusted for battle or high adventure. He was driven more by curiosity than conquest. In that, you are very different."

"What kind of stories?" Athena asked.

"He talked in the voices of characters of his own creation, imaginary friends that had come from faraway lands that he'd invented. Since he knew nothing of the real world, he created his own version of it."

"When he came to me," Prometheus began, "I had already been training orphans to prepare them for work on the sea. I'd been doing it for centuries."

"How noble of you," Athena said with a teasing smile.

"Noble, indeed," Metis said defensively. "He's trained thousands of young people over the years who had few skills otherwise."

"What led you to that calling?" Athena wanted to know, realizing that she'd never asked him.

"I wanted to spend my time at sea," he explained, "but I wanted to serve our creations in some way. I began by taking medicine and medical supplies to coastal areas in need—all over the world, but mostly along the East China, Arabian, and Mediterranean Seas. I'd buy the supplies from the wealthy regions and give them to the poorer ones. A wealthy family in Malta became benefactors. They'd been supporting an orphanage for generations. I heard about them when I offered to train a few of the older orphans from their center called the Marcella, named for their family. Years later, after my ship the *Atlantis* was no longer seaworthy, I offered to name my new ship the *Marcella* if they became permanent benefactors. They agreed."

"I wondered how it got its name," Athena remarked.

"I've grown quite close to that family," he continued. "I've known them for generations now. In fact, they know I'm a deity, and they guard that secret faithfully."

Athena tilted her head to the side. "They know you're a god?" She didn't think it wise, if he had been trying to hide from her father, to let his identity be known by those who pray to gods.

"They don't know my name," he clarified. "They know little about me—only that I have been around for a very long time. They fear and respect me. In fact, one of them thinks I'm a vampire."

Athena rolled her eyes at his joke.

"Why was your first ship called the *Atlantis*?" she asked.

"That wasn't my first ship. I've had many over the years. That was one of the first I had built and named myself."

"And you chose that name because?" Athena prodded.

"I felt like I may as well be in Atlantis, in a hidden city far away from everyone I knew and loved."

Athena frowned. All these years, she'd focused on how difficult his choice had been for her. She hadn't given enough thought to *his* suffering.

"Clymene was the one who suggested that I send Poros to Prometheus," Metis explained. "She's been watching over her son all these years and knew he was good with training young people."

Athena lifted her brows. "She knew where you were the whole time?"

Prometheus avoided her glare. "I made her swear on the River Styx to never reveal that to you."

Athena closed her eyes and sighed, wanting to remain calm for the baby.

He attempted to lighten the mood by sharing funny stories about the years he spent with Poros. While Athena enjoyed the tales, her eyes kept shifting to the opening of the chamber, expecting to see a loyalist brandishing a sword.

She wished she could reach out to Hermes and plead for his help. He'd helped her already, hadn't he? But she was too afraid to risk it. He, more than anyone she knew, loved their father.

Athena was beside herself when Prometheus kissed her and whispered, "It's time. Are you ready?"

She gave him a nod. She was terrified for their child, but she was ready.

"Oh, no," Metis said. "Clymene thinks something's wrong. She sees Selene's chariot headed this way but not close enough to the island."

Athena bit her lower lip. "If we don't go now, we'll have to wait another twenty-four hours, or come up with another plan."

"I'll make up the distance," Prometheus assured them. "Perhaps the moon goddess fears she's being watched. The cloud cover may not be enough to obscure the view for immortal eyes."

Prometheus flew with Athena through the winding tunnels to the cool, night air made thick with fog by the Nephelae.

"I don't see her," Athena whispered. "Do you?"

"Yes." Prometheus god-traveled, landing them in the sky beside Selene's silver horses.

"It's a trap!" Selene cried.

Athena noticed with horror that the goddess wore adamantine cuffs and was chained to her chariot.

From out of nowhere, an arrow pierced the throat of the moon goddess, silencing her.

"Nike!" Athena cried. To Prometheus she said, "Get me out of here."

Prometheus flew down toward the sea where the fog was thickest, but suddenly the sky was illuminated by a streak of lightning, followed by earth-shaking thunder.

Would her father strike his own daughter down?

"I'll dive into the sea," Prometheus said. "I'll take you to Poseidon's castle."

Athena clung to his neck and prepared to enter the water.

While they were still at least fifty feet from the water's surface, a lightning bolt struck the Titan square in the back. His arms went slack, as did the rest of his body, and they plunged downward until their feet were wet and Athena spurred into action. She wrapped her arms around his listless trunk and carried him away, having no idea where she was going and fearing the strain would harm her baby.

The sky lit up from another bolt headed her way. Not knowing whether she could outrun or dodge it, she screamed.

Suddenly she was scooped up and out of the way of the blast by a strong pair of arms. It was Aether, his long, white hair and beard blowing like capes behind him. In the next instant, he god-traveled with her and Prometheus, removing them from danger.

Before she could even blink, they were in a cave not much different from the one they had just left—though it was colder and less humid here.

"You're safe for the time being," he told her as they laid Prometheus on the bed.

The twin bed was beside a wooden table. There was a long couch on the other side of the table and a fire in the hearth across the room.

"Where are we?" she asked.

"Greenland, near the peak of Mont Forel."

"Near Selene's cave?"

"Yes. I saw what happened to her. I was hiding with the Nephelae."

"Thank you for rescuing us. I can't thank you enough." Tears streamed from her eyes. She slapped them away, embarrassed to appear weak.

"It's what fathers do."

When she tilted her head to the side, looking perplexed, he added, "I know he's not my son in that way, but he is in every other way."

"Of course." Then, wringing her hands, she said, "I'm hopeful that Prometheus will recover. You do believe he will recover, don't you?"

"Yes, and I have herbs that will hasten the healing. I'll brew them in a tea." Then, he noticed her belly. "Athena, are you—"

She laid her hands around the swell and smiled despite their dire circumstances. "Yes, but the child was dislodged when I shielded Prometheus from the eagle."

"If that's true, how can it be growing?"

"Apollo performed surgery to return it to my womb, but we don't know what impact that trauma had."

"Babes can be quite resilient."

Athena smiled again, pleased by his faith. "When the lightning bolt struck Prometheus, I felt it move."

"A good sign, indeed. I'll make you some of my special tea, too."

"Thank you, Aether." More tears flooded her eyes as she took a seat on the long couch opposite the bed and table. "How could my own father strike us down like that?"

"In the same way his father tried to bring harm to him. And, in more recent years, his grandfather."

"Your son, Uranus."

"Some deities—and men, too—get a lust for power that overwhelms everything else in their lives. Try not to take it personally, my dear. It's a sickness, that's what it is. It has nothing to do with love."

Athena stretched out on the couch, trying to calm herself for the sake of the baby. She prayed to her mother and Clymene with an update, letting them know they were momentarily safe. "How long before my father and his followers discover us?"

"My mountain is heavily warded and guarded by the Nephelae. I also have defensive traps positioned around the perimeter made from adamantine."

"I thought only my father had access to adamantine. Isn't it rare?"

"It is, but I hoarded it centuries ago when Prometheus was first chained to Mount Ida. I used to experiment with ways to corrode it, break it, destroy it. I eventually discovered that although it could not be destroyed, it could be reshaped. I spent decades forging keys to unlock his chains. Nothing worked, as you know."

"If you were willing to risk everything for him, why didn't you just shoot the eagle?"

"As long as Prometheus was a prisoner, I feared the repercussions for him. I wanted him free."

Athena nodded, seeing the wisdom in the god's actions.

Then, he added, his voice wavering, "I'm ashamed to admit that I eventually gave up. I'll never forgive myself for abandoning him."

With a trembling hand, Aether served her tea in a golden goblet. Then he raised a second goblet to Prometheus's lips. Athena wasn't sure what to say in response to his confession. She supposed everyone had a breaking point. He had reached his, and that's all there was to it.

"You're here for him now," she finally said. "For us and for our child. I don't know where we'd be without your help."

When he met her eyes, his own were filled with tears. "I'm glad I could be of use."

CHAPTER TWENTY-TWO

Daughters

Ten long days passed in Aether's Mont Forel cave with no movement from Prometheus. Athena had never felt so helpless. She kept badgering her mother, Clymene, Apollo, and Artemis for updates on the rebellion, but they were keeping her in the dark either because they didn't want to stress her out and risk bringing harm to the baby, or because things were too dire to admit. When she asked Aether to intercede on her behalf, he claimed that he never involved himself in the affairs of the gods.

On the eleventh day, Athena had been wiping Prometheus's brow with a cool cloth and hoping to get him to drink tea when he unexpectedly blinked.

"Prometheus? My love? Can you move? Can you speak?"

He couldn't. He could only gaze back at her.

"Aether saved us. He took us to his cave. We're safe. The baby is growing. I've been feeling it move."

She noticed the slightest twitch at the corners of his mouth. He'd wanted to smile; she was sure of it. She could tell by his eyes that he was pleased by the sight of her belly. It had doubled in size again.

"Try to give him some of the tea," Aether said as he handed her a fresh cup.

The last thing she wanted was to drown her love in tea. "Can you swallow? If so, blink once for yes and twice for no."

He blinked once.

Carefully, she put the goblet to his lips and allowed some of the warm liquid to enter his mouth. She was pleased to see him swallow it down.

"Excellent," Aether said from where he bent over them. "This will speed things up."

Athena gently drizzled more of the tea into Prometheus's mouth.

Later that day, while Athena had been napping on Aether's long couch, finally able to rest now that Prometheus was conscious, she was awakened by the sound of his voice. At first, she thought she was dreaming, but she heard him call her name a second time, and she realized the voice was coming from the bed on the other side of the table from her. She opened her eyes and sat up.

"Prometheus? Did you speak?"

"He did," Aether cried with joy. "Oh, son, do it again."

"Hello, Aether," Prometheus said. "Thank you for all you've done for me and my family."

"You don't need to thank me. You know I would do anything for you."

"I'm sorry to wake you, Athena, but I've had a vision."

She climbed to her feet and went to his bedside. "Don't apologize. What is it?"

"I saw Poseidon's castle under attack. I tried to warn our allies, but I've heard nothing back and am afraid my powers are impaired."

"I'll warn them now," Athena assured him just before she sent telepathic messages to each ally.

"I also saw Aphrodite pretending to convert to our side," Prometheus said. "Warn them that she's not to be trusted."

Nodding, Athena prayed the second message out to the rebels.

"Is Poros okay?" Prometheus asked. "And the other children?"

"I've not heard otherwise," Athena said, knowing it wasn't a solid answer.

"I hate that I'm unable to help," Prometheus groaned.

"You just did," Aether pointed out.

"My love, if you hadn't shielded the baby and me from my father's blast, I can't think what might have happened." Athena rubbed her swollen belly and felt another kick. Lifting Prometheus's limp hand, she laid it on her bump. "Wait for it . . . wait for it . . . there. Did you feel that?"

"I did. How wonderful. I can't wait to meet him or her."

Suddenly, Prometheus's hand twitched.

Aether, who had been sitting on a nearby stool jumped to his feet. "Did you just move your hand?"

"The baby," Prometheus said in astonishment as he raised his hand in the air. "The baby did something, I think."

Athena furrowed her brow. "What do you mean? What did it do?"

Prometheus placed his hand on Athena's belly again, and again he twitched—this time throughout his entire body.

"She's sending jolts of power through me."

"She?" Athena's eyes widened.

"I don't know how I know it, but it's a girl, a daughter, and she's helping me."

Athena clapped her hands with joy. "Sweet baby girl, thank you! But shouldn't you reserve your power for your own health and well-being?"

A pool of warm water rushed from between Athena's legs.

"What?" she muttered, looking down at the floor and not sure what was happening.

"Your water broke," Aether said. "You're going into labor."

"I wish my mother was here," Athena lamented as anxiety coursed through her. "I've never been so frightened." At least with the eagle, she had known what to expect. Giving birth—to a possible monster amid a revolution—entailed too many unknown factors.

"We're here," Prometheus reminded her, as he sat up for the first time since they'd arrived at the cave. "Here, take my place on the bed."

Athena crawled onto the bed and lay on her back. She was happy that her baby had healed Prometheus and happy that it was alive and coming, but she was nervous about Apollo's warnings and hoped her daughter wouldn't appear grotesque. Athena would love her no matter what; it was for the child's sake that she worried.

Aether put more pillows behind her head. "It's best if you sit up."

"How do you know such things?" Prometheus asked him.

"I've been around for a very long time."

Athena felt a pain like she'd never felt before seizing her entire abdomen. If she hadn't known better, she would have believed Echidna—the half-woman, half-snake—was coiling her thick tail around her beneath the helm of invisibility.

"Oh, gods," she said beneath her breath.

"That's a contraction," Aether said. "Can you push?"

Athena prayed to her mother and was shocked when she appeared at her side.

"I'm here, darling Athena. Aether's right. You need to push."

Reassured by her mother's presence, Athena pushed. She felt the pressure between her legs become almost unbearable. Then, the pain subsided, though the pressure remained.

"Sweet Athena, you're doing great," Prometheus, beside her, said as he smoothed her hair from her face.

"Another contraction will come," her mother warned, "and when it does, push. Tell your baby to look for an opening."

"Thank you for being here, Mother." Athena squeezed her mother's hand. "It means everything to me."

"I'm sorry I couldn't get away sooner."

"Tell me news."

"Now is not the time," her mother insisted. "Focus on your child."

The pain returned as unyielding as the first time, squeezing her like a vice. "Look for an opening, sweet baby!" Athena cried out as she pushed with all her might, wanting to get it over with.

"Your baby's crowning," Metis said from the foot of the bed. "I see its head."

"Her head," Prometheus corrected. "It's a daughter."

The pain subsided again, and Athena caught her breath. Aether brought a cool, wet cloth and placed it on her forehead. It helped to calm her down so she could breathe.

But the pain came faster this time, and harder. Athena pushed and grunted and felt movement from between her legs.

"She's coming!" Prometheus cried.

Athena pushed with all her might.

"Here she comes!" Prometheus said. "Oh, she's beautiful, Athena! She's perfect!"

"Let me see," Athena pleaded, needing to witness it herself to believe it.

Her mother cut the umbilical cord and handed over the baby, still covered in Athena's blood.

Athena held her daughter in her arms as tears slipped down her cheeks. She was perfect. It was true. The baby wriggled and opened her eyes. They were gray like Athena's.

"Hello, sweet girl," Athena said as sobs of joy caught in her throat.

"What will you call her?" Aether asked.

Athena turned to Prometheus. "Penelope, after Odysseus's wife. She was faithful and loyal and clever to the end."

"Penelope it is," Prometheus agreed with a grin.

"A beautiful name, indeed," Metis approved.

Prometheus held out his hands. "May I hold her?"

Reluctantly, Athena gave the baby to him. Joy bloomed in her heart as she watched him gaze lovingly at their child.

"Darling Penelope," he cooed. "I never thought I'd be a father."

Now that the baby was here and was a part of Athena's reality, her mind began to churn. What kind of life could the child have in a world where the gods were at odds with one another? Her own father had tried to strike Athena down and had threatened to swallow Demeter, one of his most loyal supporters.

Another wave of pain gripped her body, stunning her.

"The placenta," Metis explained. "You need to push it out."

Athena did as her mother said and was relieved when it was over, but her mind continued to reel. How safe was Penelope in such a world?

"Please don't tell the others of her existence," Athena suddenly blurted out. "Except for Clymene, let's keep her our secret."

Athena reached her arms out for the baby.

As Prometheus handed Penelope back to her mother, he asked, "But why? Why don't you want the others to know?"

"To keep her safe," Athena explained. "It's too dangerous right now. Let's make the others believe she was dead at birth—just until this revolution is resolved."

"But that could take years," Prometheus pointed out. "How will we hide her from the other gods?"

"You hid from us for centuries," Athena argued.

"But she's a child," Prometheus objected.

"She'll grow much more quickly than a human one," Metis put in. "I think Athena's right. I kept Poros hidden for the same reason."

"But your cave has been compromised," Prometheus reminded Metis. "Where will we shelter her?"

"Here," Aether offered. "You can hide her here."

Athena gawked. "Really? But you said you never interfere with the affairs of gods."

"You aren't just any gods," he assured her. "You're family. Besides, we have the Nephelae to help us."

Some of the clouds had crept into the cave to have a look at the newborn babe.

Athena exchanged a smile with Prometheus.

A New Dawn

Five years had passed since Athena gave birth to her daughter Penelope amid chaos and revolution. The war that had raged across the realms had finally subsided, leaving in its wake a new era of peace and hope. Zeus had eventually betrayed too many of his supporters to hold up against the growing rebellion, and soon all of them except Hera had turned on him—even Hermes and Ares. Now Zeus and Hera were imprisoned in the Titan Pit, albeit a much-improved version compared to the one under Zeus's rule.

Athena had pardoned many of the Titans who'd been imprisoned there, including Prometheus's father and brothers. Clymene was transformed by the return of her family. She'd already been beautiful, but everyone noticed the difference. With Aether's blessing, Athena refused to pardon Kronos and Uranus, because as Aether had once explained, they, like Zeus, belonged to that group of men and deities whose lust for power was a sickness and they therefore could not be reformed.

With only a handful of Titans, Zeus and Hera lived decent lives in the pit, which Athena outfitted with comfortable furniture and modern technology. They had access to books, television, music, and the Internet. She imagined they felt as she once did when she was trapped inside her father—comfortable but restless. From time to time, Athena and some of her siblings would deign to visit. But between her responsibilities as the new leader of the Olympians and her duties to her people, not to mention her marriage and family life, Athena was too busy to see her father often.

As the new leader of the Olympian council, Athena embraced her role with what she hoped was grace and wisdom. Drawing upon the lessons learned during the rebellion, she sought to foster a spirit of cooperation among the gods, bridging the divides that had once threatened to tear them apart. She was surprised by how quickly she was able to accomplish this. Her relationship with Hermes, for example, seemed to naturally ease back into the same rhythm it had previously possessed.

With Metis and Clymene by her side, Athena guided Olympus into a new era of prosperity, where every voice was heard and every life cherished.

But Athena's duties as a goddess were only part of her life now. As a mother to Penelope, she discovered a joy unlike any other, watching with pride as her daughter grew and thrived under her loving gaze. Balancing her godly responsibilities with her motherly ones was no easy task, but Athena approached each challenge with the same determination that had defined her throughout her life.

From the moment Penelope had entered their lives, Athena and Prometheus knew that their world had forever changed. The love they shared blossomed even further with the addition of their daughter, binding them together in a bond that transcended Athena's expectations. Despite the challenges they faced, their family stood strong, a beacon of resilience and perseverance in a world still healing from the scars of war.

Whether due to Apollo's healing touch during surgery, or Aether's special tea during Athena's pregnancy, Penelope was born with extraordinary healing powers and had become known as the goddess of healing. In five years, she was a fully grown and powerful goddess. Amphisbaena was her constant companion. Athena was often overcome with joy to see her daughter flying with Amphisbaena over Athens to answer a mortal's prayer for healing.

Meanwhile, Prometheus had found his own path to fulfillment as the captain of his ship, the *Marcella II*. His other ship, the *Marcella*, had been ravished by war, but he commissioned a new one to be built within a year of its destruction. With Poros as his first mate, they sailed the seas with a sense of purpose, taking medicine and supplies to distant lands in need while forging new alliances in the name of peace. Though their adventures often took them far from home, Prometheus always made sure to return to Athena and Penelope, his heart forever anchored to theirs.

Nights on Mount Olympus were filled with laughter and warmth, as Athena and Penelope waited eagerly for Prometheus to return from his voyages. When he arrived, weary but smiling, they would gather around the hearth, sharing stories of their day and reveling in the simple joys of family.

"Tell me about the stars, Papa," Penelope would say, her eyes wide with wonder as she listened to Prometheus's tales of the celestial wonders he had seen on his travels.

Poros often joined them, too, and as the fire crackled merrily in the hearth, he would regale them with fantastic stories of distant galaxies and far-off worlds, his words weaving a tapestry of magic and wonder that filled their hearts with joy.

But it was on Prometheus's ship that Prometheus and Athena's bond truly flourished, away from the demands of Olympus and the expectations of others. There, beneath the boundless night sky, they were free to be themselves, unburdened by the weight of their divine heritage.

In those quiet moments, as they sailed across the open sea, Athena and Prometheus found solace in each other's arms, their love a beacon of hope in a world still finding its way.

"Are you ever afraid, Athena?" Prometheus asked one night, his voice barely a whisper as they stood together on the deck of the *Marcella II*, the stars glittering overhead like diamonds in the sky.

"Afraid of what?" Athena replied, her hand reaching out to intertwine with his, their fingers fitting together like pieces of a puzzle.

"Of losing what we have," Prometheus answered softly, his gaze locked with hers as they stood together beneath the vast expanse of the night sky.

Athena smiled, her heart overflowing with love for the Titan who stood before her, his strength and courage a constant source of inspiration.

"As long as we have each other, we can face anything that comes our way," she said, her voice filled with conviction as she leaned in to press a gentle kiss against his lips. "Remember? I was once content to endure the eagle if I could be at your side."

"I remember all too well."

And so, as dawn broke on a new day, Athena looked out upon the world with hope in her heart, knowing that no matter what the future held, she would face it with the ones she loved by her side. For in the end, it was not the battles won or the empires built that mattered, but the love shared between a mother, a father, and their daughter—a love that would endure for all eternity and would help them better serve the humans in their care.

***

THE END

Acknowledgments

While I am grateful to all readers for choosing to read my books, I'm especially grateful to the following premium members for their support:

Ginger Baird
Lori Brooks
Teri Brower
Jennah Chantry
Theresa Christ
Rebekka and Sherry Colegrove
Amanda Ecker
Kerry and Kelly Erickson
Jessica Garza
Venette Grisham
Samie Hall-Rood
Patricia Hand
Misty Killion
Anita Klaboe
Leslie Lawrence
Samantha Lundergan
Carrie McCauley
Patrick Mitchell
Glorianna Peterson Murry
Carrington Parker
Liana Petrone
Rachel Renzo
Candy Smith

Debi Vap
Kimberly Walls
Kristi Yates

About the Author

Eva Pohler is a *USA Today* bestselling author of over thirty-five novels in multiple genres, including supernatural mysteries, thrillers, and young adult paranormal romance based on Greek mythology. Her books have been described as "addictive" and "sure to thrill"—*Kirkus Reviews*.

To learn more about Eva and her books, to receive a free ebook, and to sign up to hear about new releases and sales, please visit her website at https://www.evapohler.com.

Made in the USA
Monee, IL
21 April 2024

57207062R00125